"There's always that between us, isn't there?" Mikhail asked.

"I don't know what you mean." He was standing too close, and whatever pulsed hot and alive between them burned Ellie's skin. Her senses tingled. "If you weren't so afraid—"

The world stilled around them. "Of what am I afraid?" he asked very slowly.

"You're afraid to get involved. Anyone can see that."

"Can they?" he asked darkly, studying her with that close, burning intensity that seemed to make the sand shiver beneath her shoes. The waves seemed to slow and stop, the fog stilling and intimate, and Ellie could only hear the sound of her quickening heartbeat.

Then, with a rough, reluctant sigh, he tugged her to him and took her mouth with enough heat to make her forget everything but taking as he was taking....

Everything that she had sensed hidden beneath Mikhail's cold exterior was just beneath the surface, hot and real, and it was hers at last.

"So now it has begun," he whispered.

Dear Reader,

Spring into the new season with six fresh passionate, powerful and provocative love stories from Silhouette Desire.

Experience first love with a young nurse and the arrogant surgeon who stole her innocence, in *USA TODAY* bestselling author Elizabeth Bevarly's *Taming the Beastly MD* (#1501), the latest title in the riveting DYNASTIES: THE BARONES continuity series. Another *USA TODAY* bestselling author, Cait London, offers a second title in her HEARTBREAKERS miniseries—*Instinctive Male* (#1502) is the story of a vulnerable heiress who finds love in the arms of an autocratic tycoon.

And don't miss RITA® Award winner Marie Ferrarella's *A Bachelor and a Baby* (#1503), the second book of Silhouette's crossline series THE MOM SQUAD, featuring single mothers who find true love. In *Tycoon for Auction* (#1504) by Katherine Garbera, a lady executive wins the services of a commitment-shy bachelor. A playboy falls in love with his secretary in *Billionaire Boss* (#1505) by Meagan McKinney, the latest MATCHED IN MONTANA title. And a Native American hero's fling with a summer-school teacher produces unexpected complications in *Warrior in Her Bed* (#1506) by Cathleen Galitz.

This April, shower yourself with all six of these moving and sensual new love stories from Silhouette Desire.

Enjoy!

Joan Marlow Golan

Joan Marlow Golan
Senior Editor, Silhouette Desire

Please address questions and book requests to:
Silhouette Reader Service
U.S.: 3010 Walden Ave., P.O. Box 1325, Buffalo, NY 14269
Canadian: P.O. Box 609, Fort Erie, Ont. L2A 5X3

CAIT LONDON

INSTINCTIVE MALE

Published by Silhouette Books
America's Publisher of Contemporary Romance

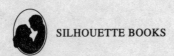

SILHOUETTE BOOKS

ISBN 0-373-76502-9

INSTINCTIVE MALE

Copyright © 2003 by Lois Kleinsasser

All rights reserved. Except for use in any review, the reproduction
or utilization of this work in whole or in part in any form by any
electronic, mechanical or other means, now known or hereafter
invented, including xerography, photocopying and recording, or in
any information storage or retrieval system, is forbidden without
the written permission of the editorial office, Silhouette Books,
300 East 42nd Street, New York, NY 10017 U.S.A.

All characters in this book have no existence outside the imagination of
the author and have no relation whatsoever to anyone bearing the same
name or names. They are not even distantly inspired by any individual
known or unknown to the author, and all incidents are pure invention.

This edition published by arrangement with Harlequin Books S.A.

® and TM are trademarks of Harlequin Books S.A., used under license.
Trademarks indicated with ® are registered in the United States Patent
and Trademark Office, the Canadian Trade Marks Office and in other
countries.

Visit Silhouette at www.eHarlequin.com

Printed in U.S.A.

Books by Cait London

Silhouette Desire

Silhouette Books

Silhouette Yours Truly

CAIT LONDON

is an avid reader and an artist who plays with computers and maintains her Web site, http://caitlondon.com. Her books reflect her many interests, including herbs, driving cross-country and photography. A national bestselling and award-winning author of category romance and romantic suspense, Cait has also written historical romances under another pseudonym. Three is her lucky number; she has three daughters, and her life events have been in threes. Cait says, "One of the best perks about this hard work is the thrilling reader response."

To Joan. Thank you.

One

Mikhail Stepanov was the one man Ellie Lathrop did not want to ask for anything.

At eight o'clock on a late February night, fog curled seductively around the Washington State coastal road; it was treacherous with curves and damp with the drizzling rain that had been falling all day. Ellie tightened her hands on the mini-station wagon's steering wheel and glanced at the sleeping child in the back seat, nestled amid her favorite blanket and toys.

The drive from Albuquerque was draining, requiring stops at rest areas for Tanya to play. A few hours at night were spent sleeping in the well-lit parking lots of restaurants because motels would have taken the last of Ellie's money. In the last six months, she had spent most of her reserves in traveling from place to place, always moving, keeping Tanya safe. Ellie drove skillfully, carefully, more so than if she had been traveling by herself—because nothing could happen to her legally adopted, precious child.

Her sister's biological child...and now Hillary wanted Tanya back, to use as a pawn in her marriage game.

Ellie ran her hand through her hair and realized she was shaking, running on coffee, nerves and fear.

Just over four years ago, she had cruised down this same twisting road, determined to irritate stern man of steel Mikhail Stepanov. Ellie's father owned the chain of Mignon International Resorts, to which Mikhail's Amoteh Resort belonged; as the boss's daughter, she often stayed at the various resorts free of charge. She had driven a sleek custom-ordered red sports car then, and fresh from a luxurious European spa, she had been up to battling Mikhail—one of her most enjoyable diversions, pricking at his meticulous businessman exterior, trying to find the man beneath. Back then, she didn't care what he thought of her, and it was all a game.

One tilt of that arrogant head, one slash of those green eyes, and her instincts told her to cut the Ice Man down a notch. Maybe back then she'd had to make him pay for being so like her father, focused on business, untouchable in his emotions.

Her father's files were complete—Mikhail Stepanov had been divorced five years ago, refusing his wife's demand to leave plans for the Amoteh Resort. JoAnna had come to Mignon's main offices and had told Paul Lathrop everything—including that she'd deliberately aborted Mikhail's baby. And yet, Mikhail revealed nothing of the emotions that would disturb another man.

Ellie's taunting games had stopped when she had became a mother to her sister's biological child. Tanya, just four years old, had to be protected, and Mikhail was the only man who could help. At six-foot three inches, he towered over Ellie's five-foot-seven frame, and when he was nearby, her instincts as a woman prickled. She refused to be intimidated by those narrowed green eyes, that forbidding scowl of dark brown brows.

Her windshield wipers click-clacked as Ellie thought of

Mikhail Stepanov, the man she must face. With a Russian immigrant father and a Texas beauty as his mother, Mikhail was devoted to his family and to the Amoteh Resort. As manager, he moved through the luxurious corridors like a lord cruising his fortress, frighteningly efficient, quiet, dark and dangerous. Always perfectly groomed and dressed in a suit, his dark brown hair neatly clipped, Mikhail was about as approachable as an iceberg. Maybe that was why she had loved taunting him so much—just to see if he was human…to see what ran beneath that steely surface.

Mikhail had the unique ability to challenge her at a level that made her want to taunt him, to bring out the real man. Her senses told her that beneath Mikhail's perfectly groomed, civilized suit lurked a primitive, sensual male—one she wanted to taste and captivate before moving on.…

A woman whose mother had deserted her as an infant and who had been raised by a cold, hurtful father, Ellie wasn't one to stay in relationships that could hurt.

Mikhail couldn't be hurt. Not once in eleven years since she'd first met him in her father's offices did he disprove her appraisal. He'd been married and divorced in that time and so had she, but whatever nettled her about Mikhail hadn't changed.

Ellie doubted that Mikhail had any personal weaknesses—the man was all steel and business, the same ilk as her father.

Her lips pressed tightly as she watched the windshield wipers smear wet trails across the glass. It was dangerous for her to attempt to pit Mikhail against Paul Lathrop—she could lose. Correction: Tanya could lose.

On the hill overlooking the small town of Amoteh, Ellie slowed the small station wagon and stopped briefly. Located on the Pacific edge of southwest Washington State, the town had taken its name from the Chinook word for strawberry, *amoteh.* The lights of the tourist town, now wrapped in rain and fog, glowed eerily in the distance.

Mikhail had fought Paul, persuading him to finance a

Mignon resort in the slow-moving, quiet town. The battles weren't sweet, but Paul had known that Mikhail's determination would find finances to create the Amoteh Resort—Mikhail's beloved "baby."

Those battles convinced Ellie that Mikhail could protect Tanya from her grandfather and irresponsible mother.

Ellie shivered, despite the warmth of the mini-station wagon. Her nails, no longer long, buffed and glossed, were now short and practical as they tightly gripped the steering wheel. *She despised her helplessness, the desperation that had made her contact Mikhail Stepanov.*

As her resources dwindled, she'd been wrangling with Mikhail, trying to nudge him into welcoming her and Tanya at the resort; Lathrops always had free accommodations. Then, six months ago, she'd been desperate. She'd ordered him to reserve a suite for her, with one room prepared for a child. After the first telephone volley between them, he hadn't answered her telephone calls, e-mails or faxes. Because she had nowhere else to send Tanya's toys, she had sent them to the Amoteh Resort.

As her father's daughter, Ellie knew how to bully and maneuver. Begging would be new and humiliating. At thirty-six years old, she was forced to deal with a man just like her father, to make concessions, to be at the mercy of his decisions.... In Mikhail's tersely expressed opinion, she was a playgirl, a jet-setter without responsibilities, legendary for her whims and parties, and she had botched a major project for the Mignon chain.

She'd botched nothing, merely taken the blame for Hillary, and she wasn't that playgirl any longer; she was desperate to protect her child and nothing of her former wealth remained. Ellie tightened her hands on the steering wheel; she was done wrangling, threatening and contacting Mikhail. If she had to, she'd beg....

Rain slashed against the windshield, as cold and welcoming as Mikhail would be. Ellie brushed a tear from her cheek. She hated crying, and yet with her financial reserves and strength almost gone and danger threatening Tanya, she needed the only man who could help her keep her child...if he would.

She weighed arriving at the Amoteh Resort and facing Mikhail; Tanya shouldn't be exposed to that first clash, because they always clashed, didn't they? Mikhail in that quiet, dark, intense way as a response to her glittering, slashing offensive. She'd circled him, looking for a weakness, and had found none.

But this time, *Ellie would not let herself respond to the instincts that Mikhail always set off. She would not....*

Ellie turned the car from the Amoteh and toward the Stepanov home. She had met Mikhail's parents, Fadey and Mary Jo Stepanov, earlier, at a social dinner at the opening of the Amoteh, and had liked them instantly.

With the instinct of a mother protecting her child, Ellie drove to the Stepanov home, a bold wooden structure overlooking the Pacific Ocean.

Two hours later, Mikhail Stepanov wanted to toss Ellie Lathrop out on her expensive derriere, the one clad in black designer jeans and seated on the walnut desk in his sprawling office. As manager of the expansive Amoteh Resort, he knew how to get rid of unwanted "pests." Mikhail narrowed his eyes, considering the terms in which to best frame Ellie, and came up with "A Big Bloody Thorn in My Side, the Potential to Ruin Everything, the Woman I Wish Were Anywhere But Here." Then he added mentally, "The woman who dumped a pitcher of ice water over my head at a business meeting when I agreed with Paul, the woman who lobbed pâté across an elegant dinner table at me, the woman who brought an entire party into my bedroom at her father's house, the woman I want most to avoid."

At nine o'clock at night, the rain outside Mikhail's office window pattered softly. The Amoteh Resort, luxuriously huge and sprawling, was ominously quiet. The few off-season tourists, taking advantage of the lower rates, had settled in for the night, and the minimal staff had gone to their homes in the small, quaint oceanside town.

With a mix of rain, ice and snow expected, Mikhail would have ordinarily gone to his parents' home to meet the guest staying there. But Ellie wasn't just any guest, and he wanted their battle to be private.

Mikhail sent a pointed, narrow-eyed message to said curved bottom on his desk, and Ellie smiled blandly at him. She tilted her head just that bit that said she recognized his hint and wasn't taking it. Cut in different layers, her shoulder-length hair was sun-streaked, the tips catching the light, shifting over the darker layers beneath. A smooth strand of silky hair slid across her cheek, gleaming and catching the soft lighting. Her tan was genuine, not from a bottle. But above that soft cheek, Ellie's gray eyes were taunting and veiled by her sweeping eyelashes.

He liked order in his business and in his life, and Ellie knew exactly how to tear that order apart. He refused to let her nettle him.

Her mouth curved slightly and one fine dark eyebrow lifted, challenging him as she moved just enough to nudge a neat stack of papers. The top one slid aside and Mikhail checked himself from straightening them. She knew perfectly well that he preferred order.

All five-foot seven, sleek, selfish, spoiled inches of her, from that carefully tousled shoulder-length hair down to her neatly trimmed boots, had irritated him since the day he first met her—the boss's daughter.

"I warned you that I was coming. You've had months to prepare. I told you to get a suite ready with a room for a child," Ellie said softly in her cultured, I've Got You, Bub, Boss's Daughter tones. "I sent boxes of toys. Where are they?"

If he could have tossed Ellie out into the night, he would have. From experience, he knew that where Ellie went, she brought trouble.

In this case, she had brought trouble to his parents' home—in the form of a four-year-old girl. His parents' delight had sounded over the telephone; they were happy to baby-sit while Ellie Lathrop came to see him. The child was already tucked in and sleeping deeply after his father's bedtime stories.

Mikhail didn't want to think about whose child she was. Ellie hadn't been pregnant at the opening of the Amoteh over four years ago, and now she'd collected a four-year-old child. Paul had been silent about his daughters, but then he wasn't a sentimental man. Guessing anything about Ellie was a disaster; she was unpredictable. "The toys are in the storeroom. You can take them with you. You're not setting up camp in the Amoteh."

"Oh, I'm not?"

There was just that crisp, taunting tone that could set him on edge. How typical of her, Mikhail thought, to arrive at night. Just for the night—because in the morning, she was leaving, Paul Lathrop's daughter, or not.

"My parents called, warning me of your arrival. They said the little girl is asleep in their guestroom. That's an indication you aren't certain of your welcome at the Amoteh, and you went to my parents because you know of their softness for children. Let me clarify the situation for you— You will not use my family, Ellie, and you are not welcome here."

"Your mother and father were thrilled to baby-sit. I'm going to be staying with them, too. I'm more than welcome there, if not here. I'll be a regular part of your family. Won't that be nice?" she asked too sweetly, in the taunting tone she'd used before.

Mikhail chewed on that galling truth—his mother, Mary Jo, had been thrilled, of course…almost as delighted as Fadey, his father. Their first grandchild, Jarek Stepanov and his wife Leigh's baby, would be born in three weeks, and they had always loved children. Therefore, it made sense that Ellie chose the loving Stepanov family for her victims—a stealthy way to get to Mikhail and torture him as only she could do.

And for some unexplained reason, Mikhail's parents delighted in hearing of his clashes with Ellie. Their interest in his battles with Ellie was only exceeded by his younger brother's teasing. Jarek liked her, and before his marriage to Leigh, Jarek and Ellie had played a flirting game that they both knew would go no further. Mikhail had sensed that they did so to torment him.

His ex-wife's games and torments had made him *immune to flirtation from self-serving women like Ellie.*

Outside, the black swells of the Pacific eased to caress the shoreline, fog curling around the piers, creeping up the steps to enfold the massive Amoteh Resort, caressing it like a lover.

An offshore buoy sounded softly, warningly, as Mikhail opened the window for a breath of crisp, salt-scented air he had loved all his life. Soft lights shone in his parents' home, a jutting wood and rock structure with sprawling porches that overlooked the ocean and, a distance away, his brother Jarek's new home with Leigh.

Just north on the coastline was Strawberry Island. In another century a Hawaiian chieftain, captured and enslaved by whalers and shipwrecked on this island, had died. Bitterly alone and longing for his homeland, Kamakani had placed a curse on Strawberry Island: only a woman who knew her own heart could dance before his grave and remove that curse.

Mikhail decided that Ellie was his private curse. He'd known it from the moment he'd met her eleven years ago in Paul Lathrop's Seattle office, expensively dressed for a tennis game, and—on the company payroll—laying out her day of saunas and beauty shops and a party that night. He'd known she was a curse when the Amoteh opened and Ellie held a private party in her suite. Mikhail had been called to break up the brawl between two rich playboys competing for her favors. Playing her games, she had sent a pack of

equally spoiled women after Mikhail. Ellie had told them
that just-divorced Mikhail was on the lookout for a new
wife.

One wife of the same spoiled social set as Ellie was
enough for Mikhail. At thirty-nine years old, he had one
love—the Amoteh Resort.

He turned to Ellie and frowned slightly as she eased off
the black leather jacket she had been wearing to reveal a
buttoned-up white sweater that fitted her curves perfectly.
She arched and stretched sensuously and looked drowsily
at him.

Mikhail inhaled sharply, surprised at the impact of that
look. He jammed his hands into his pockets; they had a
sensation stirring in them—how would her breasts would
feel cupped in his hands? ''Try that on someone else,'' he
said briskly. ''I'm immune.''

She yawned and stretched again, a feminine contrast to
the heavy walnut Stepanov furniture in his office. ''I'm not
playing games with you, Mikhail. I'm too tired. But thanks
for the invitation.''

Ellie knew just where to place the barbs. ''I wasn't inviting,'' he said. ''You are not welcome at the Amoteh.''

That his parents' home was another matter grated.

She turned to him, her expression set, eyes narrowed and
glittering like steel, just as it was when she was determined
to have her way. Her word was a slashing order. ''Reconsider.''

''Not a chance. Every time you're in the vicinity, bad
things happen. There was that botched deal at the last minute—it cost Paul a prime chunk of prospective Cannes real
estate and hours of negotiation. Brawls, staff quitting, food
tossing, midnight swimming contests, that sort of thing.
You have no regard for the schedule your father's staff
must keep. This incident is an Ellie classic— You were
angry with Paul once and distracted a business meeting at
corporate headquarters in Seattle by bringing a dog fashion
show right into the conference room. He had to donate

money to the animal shelter on the spot, just to get rid of the menagerie causing havoc during an important meeting. It was simple blackmail.''

''That little Yorkie loved you and you know it.'' Ellie bared her teeth in a smile. They gleamed, all perfect and sharp. ''I promise to be good,'' she singsonged softly.

Mikhail refused to respond; he had seen Ellie in action. Paul Lathrop's daughter was a life-seasoned fighter, holding her own. She knew how to blend femininity with steel, how to cut and slash and bargain, and she always landed on her feet, taking care of herself. She might not know it, but in Paul's hard heart, he respected her. Mikhail had seen Paul and Ellie, toe to toe, in an argument, yelling, verbally hitting at each other, and she was very good at getting what she wanted.

She was not getting what she wanted this time.

She frowned slightly, her voice low, all humor erased, just stating facts, summing them up in a neat package as though she had thought carefully about each one. ''Everyone knows that you've got one thing on your agenda, and that is the perfection of the Amoteh. You've pushed Paul into putting one of his Mignon International Resorts into a bit of isolated beach with nothing to offer, off the main interstate. You're determined to make the resort succeed, drawing in trade for the townspeople, and supply the rooms with Stepanov furniture, made by your family. My father is using your setup here as a model for his other resorts—you're his star high-achiever. You're a man he respects.''

Mikhail let that remark pass. Paul's personal ethics did not agree with Mikhail's, but the owner of the worldwide resort chain was a good businessman and he could be made to listen. An orphan who came from the harsh city streets, Paul Lathrop had built a worldwide chain of resorts. Mikhail understood the desperation for respect—as an immigrant, Fadey had been desperate to prove himself worthy of Mary Jo's wealthy Texan family. ''Whatever you want—no.''

"Listen, bud," Ellie said slowly as she rose to her feet. "I'm dead tired and in no mood to present my problem in a sensitive, logical way. I need you to help me. You're the only man who can. I've tried everything else, and you're my last resort. Do you actually think I would humiliate myself in front of you if I had any other choice?"

She smiled weakly as if admitting defeat to herself, and for the first time, Mikhail noted the taut lines of her face, the fatigue shadowing her eyes. A little of the brittleness shifted into a softness he hadn't expected. "See you in the morning, bud. And try to be a little more pleasant for my daughter, will you? Tanya is an innocent in this whole mess."

Daughter. Whoever had given birth to the child, it wasn't Ellie. Mikhail remembered her body in that sleek, black maillot suit and pressed close against him as she taunted him; it wasn't maternal just over four years ago. While he was turning that thought, Ellie slowly, tiredly made her way out of his office. He followed her to the doorway and frowned when she braced a hand against the wall, slumping. She turned to the wall, placing both hands flat against it, as if she had nowhere else to go. She looked fragile and wounded and too tired to go on.

"I hate you. You're so much like him," she whispered as he came close and supported her with an arm around her waist. Without the feline arrogance she usually tossed at him, her body seemed terribly light and fragile.

And then he saw that she was crying—tough, willful, spoiled Ellie was crying. Not racking, hard sobs, but the soft sound that said she was trying to withhold her burden and couldn't.

The hair on Mikhail's nape lifted warningly. He might dislike Ellie, but he wasn't immune to a woman crying. And Ellie Lathrop never cried—she pushed and shoved and threatened and sulked and maneuvered and haunted, but she never cried.

With a sinking feeling and mental warnings flashing in

the softly lit corridor, Mikhail eased her gently into the
Stepanov Furniture display room and closed the heavy
door. Ellie seemed to sink to the massive bed created by
Fadey. With shoulders slumped, she brushed her hands
wearily against her face. In the next moment, as though she
feared he would see too much, she was on her feet, standing
taut as if held upright by strings. She smiled too brightly.
"Got to go. Talk with you in the morning."

He didn't trust her. Was this a new act? Something she'd
devised to mock him?

Mikhail could feel the tension ripping through her like
electricity. From those shadows beneath her eyes, he sur-
mised that whatever was bothering her had taken its toll.
He placed a hand on her shoulder and eased her back down
to sit on the bed. "Talk now."

"I don't want to talk now," Ellie said bluntly, tiredly.
"I'm not up to fighting with you. Give me a break, will
you?"

"No. Talk…now."

She scrubbed her hands over her face, and Mikhail noted
the absence of her usual perfect but light cosmetics—no
mascara, no glossy, sexy lips. His gaze ripped down her
body, and found, for the first time, the missing button on
the leather jacket, the slightly frayed collar of the sweater,
the worn seams of her jeans and her scuffed boots.

Ellie noted his closer inspection and turned her face
away. "I'm not at my best," she admitted shakily and sank
back down on the bed. "I'm just so tired."

What could have made her swallow her pride and come
to him? Whose child had she borne…or otherwise ac-
quired? Had the man deserted them? Mikhail folded his
arms over his chest and leaned back against the sturdy walnut armoire he had helped to build. "Tell me."

"No."

"You will." He reached to turn on an elegantly crafted
brass lamp, lightbulbs hidden in the almost realistic bouquet
of tulips. The lamp was a product of a local craftsman, just

like the woven table runners on the dining room table. Mikhail smoothed the mauve-colored glass petals with his fingertip, admiring the skill of the artist. More than one family in Amoteh depended on the resort's success and the display of their crafts. His goal was to provide work in a community he loved—and he wasn't going to let Paul Lathrop's willful daughter spoil the resources the Amoteh could provide for local artists.

In profile, Ellie's head lifted, her gray eyes shadowed into black. Even exhausted, the defiance and the skill of holding her own with a powerful man like her father was there. "I'll deal with you when I'm ready."

Mikhail didn't want the night watchman to interrupt. Ellie had brought a child to his parents and she had asked for his help. It must have cost her pride, and he had to have answers. What could have driven her away from her social set to the isolation of Amoteh? Why were her clothes worn, when Ellie had always dressed perfectly? *Who had fathered her child?*

He resented the need to know more, and his instincts told him that he should resist curiosity.

His instincts told him that she desperately needed him.

Mikhail reached to hang a Do Not Disturb sign to the outside of the showroom. Though his apartment was just down the hallway, he sometimes relaxed in this room filled with furniture his family had made. Occasionally his brother, Jarek, used the showroom to romance his wife away from their new home. The Do Not Disturb sign meant the Stepanovs were in the showroom and did not want to be disturbed. He clicked the lock on the showroom door closed. "I can wait."

"You would." Ellie was on her feet, stalking the room filled with the heavy walnut furniture. A restless woman, she stopped to smooth the wood admiringly, to open a drawer, closing it smoothly, to trace the intricate hardware of a dresser.

Mikhail dismissed the too-tense sensation prowling his

body as he watched her move gracefully, a pampered woman whose only obsession had been her own indulgences.

She turned on him like a tigress, fists clenched, her hair and body softly outlined by the lights from the parking lot. "You're amused. I see it in your expression. I don't like being your entertainment du jour. Au revoir, bud."

With that, she walked past him to the door and reached for the lock.

Mikhail studied her. Ellie Lathrop was too tense, too brittle...and she had cried. *What game was she playing?*

"Walk out that door and you're not getting a second chance." He watched her hesitate and her slender hand slid from the lock. What could be so important as to make Ellie sacrifice her pride?

Why did he want to tug her back to him, hold her safe and warm against him?

He tossed that thought aside. It was only natural for a Stepanov man to want to protect a woman in dire need.

The tingle at the back of his neck warned him that his own instincts could endanger him.

With her back to him, Ellie shook her head, and a spill of sun-lightened hair caught the soft light in sparks. "You're so much like Paul—my dear old dad. No wonder my mother left him as soon as she was able, leaving me, too, of course. My half sister's mother did the same. It seems that maternal instincts don't run in our family. You know that I'm tired—dead tired—and you're pushing. You pick others' weak moments like a shark scenting blood... anything to get your way. I should have expected no less. You're not going to make this easy."

She turned slowly, leaning back on the door, her hands behind her. In the soft lighting, her face was pale, her eyes huge and shadowed. She spoke in an uneven whisper. "I have a child. She needs protection. And you are my last resort. I'll do anything you say to keep her safe. Just help me—rather help her. If I have to beg, I will."

The honest plea in her voice struck him...a tired, desperate mother seeking shelter. She seemed to sag then, against the dark heavy wood of the door, her head down. "I can't run anymore, Mikhail. I need your help."

"Details," he demanded roughly to cover his unsteady emotions. He didn't know if he should trust this submissive Ellie. "You were married. Less than three and a half years ago, wasn't it? I received an invitation to the wedding."

"And I received your gift. Crystal, wasn't it? I forget. It brought a nice price when I sold it. I've sold a lot of things in the past few years."

He'd chosen the crystal vase because it reminded him of the woman—glittering, perfect and hard. "He's the child's father?"

She scrubbed her hands together now, as if trying to dislodge a cold that came from her bones. "I wish he were. Mark would have been a wonderful father, but he couldn't accept someone else's child. We're divorced. I took back the Lathrop name, just to torture Paul, to remind him that he does have a daughter.... Parental obligations and all that. Or let's just say I've inherited Paul's perversity. By the way, has my dear father called?"

Mikhail nodded, remembering Paul's brisk, slightly angry tone. "Several times in the past six months. He wondered where you were."

"That's why I didn't let you know that we were coming. I didn't want him to know until I'd—until I'd talked with you."

Ellie sat on the bed, shoulders slumped, and then with a sigh, settled against the back, legs outstretched. She sent him a glance that could only be labeled as resentful. "It's not easy to talk with you, you know. You don't inspire easy conversation. You give nothing away—do you have feelings, Mikhail? Do you? Or are you just made of wood, like the totem poles outside?"

A homage to the northwest Native Americans, the totem poles were huge and savagely painted masks created in wood, unsoftened by the tall pine branches enfolding them. The carved symbols represented the Hawaiian chieftain enslaved by whalers and dying far from his beloved homeland.

"I might be slightly more attractive," he said quietly and watched her frown at his dry humor.

In one of those lithe, lightening quick movements, she was on her feet and standing near him, looking up. "I'm going to do something that may frighten you, Mikhail, but I really need this."

With that, she slid against him, her arms circling his waist. She placed her face against his throat. "Could you just hold me? Just hold me, and let me feel safe and not alone for just one minute?"

Mikhail held very still, every nerve taut, warnings leaping inside him. Ellie was shivering, reminding him of a little wounded seagull he'd once found. He'd seen Ellie lean close to men before, casually, flirting with them, but this was different. This was desperation.

"What game are you playing?" he asked rawly as a soft strand of her hair brushed his lips.

Because he knew the dangers of playing with Ellie, the effects she'd had on other men, tantalizing them, he reached to move that silky, fragrant strand from his skin—the texture was too feminine, too intimate. Then, instinctively, his fingers lodged in her hair, his fist crushing that softness as he drew her face up to his.

With his other hand, he angled her face to the light. She was thinner, her cheekbones sharply defined beneath that gleaming, damp skin; her lashes had spiked, those dark haunted eyes bearing the sheen of tears. Her body still shook against his.

She dropped her arms beside her body, seeming to hang there, suspended as he studied her, his hands holding her because Ellie seemed as if she would drop when he released her. "When was the last time you slept?"

Her answer came on a ragged sigh that had to be genuine, and she closed her eyes. "Days, it seems. I napped on the way from Albuquerque."

Ellie never admitted personal weakness. She was all gloss and well-tuned, moving like a sleek tigress; he'd seen her glittering, flashing temper with Paul and playing games amid her jet-setter crowd, but not like this. A warning trickle that she might really need him frizzoned up Mikhail's nape. "You're thinner. Are you sick? Do you want something to eat…drink?"

"I'm not hungry." Her lashes fluttered, as if she were trying to open her lids, and her words were no more than a sigh. "I'm so tired, Mikhail. Can we discuss this in the morning?"

Okay, so he felt like a brute, demanding answers of an exhausted woman. That's what JoAnna had called him, wasn't it? *A low-class, cold brute without a drop of anything to make a woman happy.*

Mikhail released Ellie's silky hair at once. His other hand, cradling her upturned face, contrasted with that fine light skin, and he frowned as he noticed his thumb caressing the texture. He jerked his hand away and Ellie seemed to sag, her shoulders drooping. She didn't move, her eyes closed, as if too tired to think, to taunt.

"We're expecting a mix of weather tonight. It's already started to snow, and the road back to my parents' house is probably iced by now. You can sleep here. My parents will take care of the child. We need to finish this discussion," Mikhail said roughly, surprising himself as he swept back the lush purple comforter to the fresh black sheets and the featherbed beneath. He turned off the lamp, but the rain on the windows caught light, seducing soft flowing pools into the room.

Ellie didn't move.

"Ellie?" he asked softly, turning her to him.

Her eyes were open now, but not seeing. He knew that look; she was already asleep on her feet. Mikhail took a deep breath and helped her out of her jacket, tossing it onto a heavily built chair. "Sit," he said and when she didn't move, he eased her onto the bed, then kneeled to untie her boots.

The worn shoelaces had been knotted instead of replaced, the toes of the boots were scuffed.

Then she was tilting, eyes closed, already sleeping deeply before her head touched the pillow. Mikhail slid her boots from her feet and noted the worn, mismatched socks before stripping them away. He eased her legs up onto the bed and covered her.

Ellie snuggled into the luxurious featherbed and comforter with a sigh. Suddenly, she sat up, her eyes pleading with him. "Mikhail? Mikhail, you'll see that Tanya is okay, won't you? She wakes up at night, and she needs to know that I'm with her."

She threw back the coverlet as though fear drove her. "I've got to go. She'll need me."

What fear could drive her so desperately? Mikhail recognized an exhausted mother who would give her last for her child. The image did not suit what he knew of Ellie. "If she needs you, my mother will call. You're staying here."

"You promise that she'll call?" She sounded like a sleepy, hopeful child and not like the willful Ellie he'd known.

"Of course," he returned with an arrogance typical of the Stepanov males. "I have said so, have I not?"

"Of course. When you say that, I know…." With a slight smile, Ellie allowed herself to be tucked in again. She was soundly sleeping within minutes, and Mikhail was left with an uneasy sense that he was susceptible to her. *What could have driven her so hard, so desperately, to him?*

Asleep, one hand by her face, her hair splayed across the black satin pillowcase, she looked like a vulnerable child, her lips slightly parted.

No, she looked like an inviting woman and trouble, and

after experiencing his ex-wife, he'd already had his share of spoiled society women. Mikhail jammed his hands into his slacks pockets, resenting the sensual tug Ellie could always draw from him. The need to hold all that fire in his hands, to possess her in a storm that would wash him free of her.

Or would it?

Two

Ellie awoke slowly, stretching and enjoying the smooth feel of the sheets along her bare skin. Was she really sleeping, cramped in her car and dreaming? Or was she awake and the big warm bed and the crackling warmth of a fire real?

A hard slash of sleet on the windows tore her from sleep. She sat up, already fearing for Tanya—who wasn't anywhere near. Ellie could feel the bone-chilling fear seeping into her, despite the warmth of the featherbed. For six months, she'd been running to keep Tanya safe, and now—

Mikhail Stepanov was there. On top of the coverlet and sleeping beside her, Mikhail's arm crossed her lower stomach. His big hand had curled possessively on her hip.

Ellie jerked the comforter up to her throat and shook her head slightly, trying to dislodge the nightmare. Still, Mikhail lay big and solid beside her in the high sturdy bed, his meticulous dress shirt opened halfway down his chest, his long legs sheathed in slacks, his feet bare. Stubble was beginning to darken his jaw, and he did not look civilized at all, not with the firelight flickering over that hair on his chest, those tousled dark waves.

She breathed quietly, trying to bridge the unsteady gap between deep sleep and Mikhail in a bed beside her. Her bare skin and the lacy white drift of cloth tossed on a sturdy bedside table told her that she was wearing only briefs. She summed up the situation: She was in bed with Mikhail, wearing very little. And she was very much awake.

One more heartbeat and Ellie closed her eyes in relief; Tanya was safe, sleeping at Fadey Stepanov's house.

When she opened her eyes again, the bold sturdy furniture in the room reminded her that this was the Stepanov showroom. In the dim light, the bold, almost primitive style was unmistakable. Behind a huge brass fireguard, a fire blazed, warming and lighting the room, catching the textures of cloth and wood and dancing on the metal. Above the massive stone fireplace, a thick mantel of smoothly polished walnut wood bore pictures in gleaming assorted frames. Mikhail's business jacket and tie were meticulously placed over the back of one of the matching big wood chairs near the fire. His highly polished shoes gleamed on the woven rug circling the chairs, and pottery marked with the Amoteh's strawberry logo sat on a food tray.

Brochures gleamed on the long woven scarlet runner crossing a bold dining room table with matching chairs. The rich colors of cloth, purple and red, were almost savage, cutting across the dark wood. The thick slabs of blood-red cushions softened the bold, blocky style. The black throw pillows had been crushed, suggesting that Mikhail had sat there for a time.

The big hand on her hip caressed, and Ellie watched, frozen and fascinated, as Mikhail's fingers opened and dug into the lush purple material—and pressed deep to lock onto her flesh.

In that moment, she knew that whatever Mikhail wanted, he would possess and keep.

He breathed heavily, just that once, and her skin prickled in warning. Mikhail sharp and untouchable in a business suit was one thing; this man was another.

This aroused man, she corrected as her eyes swept down his body and the coastal wind slashed the rain against the windows. The sound of wind and rain was almost as primitive as Mikhail looked now.

She'd felt this way before with Mikhail, but never so sharply. The stirring within her was that of a huntress finding exactly what she wanted and pitting herself against a man in the most elemental of ways, stripping away all else and battling until she had filled whatever need drove her. As a natural competitor, she wanted to throw herself at him, nothing withheld, she was overwhelmed by that very irritating physical need to dominate Mikhail's arrogance.

And yet Ellie feared what would happen if ever they really clashed, because Mikhail was definitely up to any battles.

Her senses prickled, every nerve in her body went taut and she looked up quickly. Those drowsy green eyes were watching her, those of a predator, and his voice was deep and slow, like that of a sleepy lover. "It's three o'clock. I called my parents. They know you're not coming back tonight. Go back to sleep. We'll talk in the morning."

Mikhail's image now didn't suit her "Ice Man" label for him. That he was a man now and not encased in ice and steel terrified her. He looked as if she could turn to him and—

Ellie's protective instincts leaped; she'd learned not to trust her softer instincts as a woman. "I'm not sleeping in this bed with you, and you had no right to undress me."

He sighed heavily and slid his hand from her to place it with the other behind his head. His expression was that of drowsy interest and humor. "You're not completely undressed. You're wearing briefs. Beige, I think, cut high on the thigh. Cotton, not lace. One sizable hole on the left cheek. And I didn't touch you."

She tugged the coverlet to raise it over her bare shoulders, but Mikhail's weight declined the favor. She refused to ask, choosing a demand to cover her uncertainty. "Move...off...this bed."

Mikhail's eyebrows rose slightly, mocking her. They both knew she was at the disadvantage, and not in any position to order him. He spoke too softly, his deep voice grating on her senses. "I want to get to the bottom of this, why you're here. Now. Tonight. Do we talk here, or by the fire while you eat, or are you going back to sleep?"

"How did I get undressed then? Exactly how do you know what briefs I'm wearing?" she pressed furiously, humiliated that she had exposed her body to him. The purchase of new underwear wasn't possible, and she didn't like Mikhail seeing how destitute she had become. Despite what he thought of her, only her ex-husband had seen her undressed and even then, she'd been shy and self-protective—wary of exposure and criticism.

Was that pleasure in the slight curve of his hard mouth? "I was resting by the fire, minding my own business, with a little paperwork and some food, when you threw back the covers, stood and undressed. Your clothes are right where you dropped and threw them. I'm not your maid."

She stared at him, and he reached to press a fingertip beneath her jaw, lifting slightly. "You can close your mouth now."

That dark gaze was roaming over her mussed hair, her face unshielded by cosmetics, and lower to her mouth and still lower, over her bare shoulders. Mikhail was studying her like a man interested in her as a woman. She shivered and realized that color was slowly rising in her cheeks. Ellie turned away, not wanting him to see so deeply inside her, to know that intense male assessment could terrify her.

The bed jarred as Mikhail suddenly stood up. He impatiently tore off his shirt as if no longer interested in her, tossing it onto the bed. "Put this on. We're not going anywhere tonight and Tanya is safe and sleeping. Since you are awake, now is the best time to talk without interruption. Come by the fire and eat.''

There was the slightest roughness to his voice, the inherited trace of Fadey's Russian accent, as Mikhail turned his back to her. He walked to the fire, crouching to prod it into a blaze.

Ellie slid into his shirt, buttoning it firmly. When she began to roll up the sleeves, she caught his scent—underlying the soap and starch of the cloth, his personal scent warned and stormed around her. Wary of this new Mikhail, she watched the movements of his powerful shoulders, the firelight gleaming on them. He stood, hands on hips, watching the fire, a big powerful man who held his family…and his precious resort safe.

Ellie smoothed the large shirt around her. Maybe it was just her fantasy, her hope, her desperation, but just wearing Mikhail's shirt made her feel safer.

He was just the man she needed, and clearly she would have to play this game his way. She cautioned herself to be patient, not her best quality.

Ellie slid from the high bed and reached for the only softness in the room, a dull gun-metal green fringed shawl placed over a dresser. The flight of the last six months ached in her bones; exhaustion dragged and sucked at her, the warmth of the bed calling her now. Once in it, she didn't doubt that she could sleep for a week—if Tanya were safe. In the past, Ellie would have loved pitting herself against Mikhail. Now the battle to convince him seemed overwhelming, a grudging step-by-step uphill battle to get him to commit to Tanya's safety.

She wrapped the shawl around her waist, knotting it.

She didn't do well at her first attempt to ask Mikhail to help; he'd set her off too easily. Just seeing him, so confident and disdainful of her, she'd felt that instinctive need to prod those cold, aloof shields.

Ellie couldn't afford to fail a second time. She couldn't fail Tanya; she had to be alert for Mikhail's agile mind.

Inhaling deeply, she braced herself to convince Mikhail and walked to the fireplace.

His body seemed to tense, though he hadn't moved, and that flick of his eyes took in her bare leg, exposed by the shawl's fringes.

Ellie tried to ignore the leap of her senses, because now she couldn't afford her habit of nettling Mikhail. She concentrated on the mantel's pictures, gathering as much calm as she could. The hair on her nape lifted as it always did when Mikhail was nearby, and she could almost feel him breathe, waiting for her to talk.

Not just yet. She had to be very careful this time.

From their gold frame, the immigrant Stepanov brothers, dressed in peacoats and knitted caps, stared back at her—tough, unflinching, determined, with the same wide and uncompromising jaw and slashing cheekbones as Mikhail. In another frame, softly ornate, a young Fadey beamed as he held a blissfully happy Mary Jo in her wedding dress. Then the young brothers, Mikhail and Jarek, looking wild and free as the ocean wind tossed their hair, huge fishing poles in one hand and holding aloft strings of fish in their other hands. In the photograph, the ocean waves crested behind them.

"Eat," Mikhail said simply when she came to stand beside him, though he didn't turn. The firelight played on his face, lighting the jutting angles and escaping the hard planes. He had set the terms already, the schedule by which she must perform, make her plea.

She'd learned terms and prices at an early age, from her father. Everything was a trade-off, wasn't it? she thought wearily.

Ellie eased into a chair near the food and wished that her stomach hadn't just growled. Obviously, Mikhail was not playing waiter. She opened the thermos bottle and inhaled the delicious scent of chowder, easing it into the large pottery soup bowl. She carefully unwrapped the thick slabs of dark bread, heavily slathered with butter. In another moment, she was diving into the food, forgetting about Mikhail. She was halfway through the soup before Mikhail reached to open the other thermos bottle, pouring milk into her glass.

"Thanks." For now it was delicious food, no matter who was serving it. She crushed crackers into the soup, mixed rapidly and hurried to eat the savory creamy mix of clams and potatoes.

The impact of the hot food and the warmth of the fire had made her drowsy again. With little effort, she could lean back against the chair's cushion and sleep—but she couldn't; she couldn't fail Tanya.

Mikhail sat, leaning back on the chair, his legs in front of the fire as he studied the flames. In profile, his rugged features looked too primitive, the light flickering over his chest and arms. In a suit, he looked powerful and sleek and untouched by emotion. But now, he seemed even stronger, more potent—more elemental, from his broad shoulders to the slight matting of hair on his chest that veed downward.

Ellie tensed as she remembered awakening to him, the soft beckoning of her senses to smooth his skin, to touch and hold all that male power within her hand.... He'd been aroused. A little quiver shot deep within her; it was difficult to think of Mikhail as a man with ordinary needs.

"Finished?" he asked softly.

"Yes, it was delicious. Did I thank you?" She struggled against sleep; she needed to be alert to ask Mikhail's help.

"Of course." There was the old-world arrogance, as if he had momentarily relaxed his shields with her. "Now tell me why you have been sleeping with the child, singing to her and holding her tight against you?"

Ellie's drowsy senses snapped to alert. "How do you know that?"

Mikhail turned to her and said slowly, "Because it was me you held in your arms, Ellie. Me you rocked and petted and reassured in your sleep. The experience was unique, to say the least."

* * *

While Ellie stared at him, wide-eyed, her lips parted, Mikhail dealt with his unsteady emotions. The big, chunky chair only served to make her more feminine, more vulnerable. He resented the woman in front of him, all curves and soft lips, the shawl tied around her waist opening to reveal long smooth legs. His hand flexed, remembering the jut of her hip, the curve of her waist beneath the thick comforter.

Ellie Lathrop was a disaster, his personal Kamakani curse. His instinctive need to have her wear his shirt, to claim her as his, nettled.

He was not an emotional man, yet what man would not be affected by a woman's bare breasts pressed against his arm, those little affectionate hugs, and those soft lips kissing his shoulder and whispering in the night, "Go to sleep, baby. I'm right here and I'll never leave you."

"Rock-A-Bye Baby" had never been so erotic, the husky, sleepy sound of Ellie's voice making him hard— and weak. Despite himself, he could not move when she curled so close to him, her hands stroking his skin, cuddling him, her body scent reaching inside his senses, tormenting him. Yet, as much as he knew the danger of staying, he could not leave her. Instead, he resented the fine sheen of perspiration on his skin, the sensual tension humming through him.

Mikhail scoffed at himself and was surprised at the hard, derisive snort that could only have come from himself. *Him. Hard. Aching to take her. Aroused by Ellie, the spoiled, willful heiress.*

What could have happened to a child that she would need such reassurance in the night?

"You will tell me now about the child and why you have come." That his accent had slipped beyond his control also nettled. The fact that the shawl had shifted slightly, revealing an enticing thigh, golden and gleaning in the firelight, hit him like a physical blow.

He wanted to press his lips to that soft flesh. He wanted to toss her on that bed and fight out the storm brewing between them for years.

What would that solve? his logical, nonaroused side demanded. They would still be the same people, each disliking the other.

He'd battled another woman, and that experience with his ex-wife had been enough to turn his sexual needs cold.

There was no reason for Ellie to excite him, none at all, and yet she did.

He watched Ellie pull into herself, the sleepy vulnerability gone. She ran her fingers through her hair and sipped the milk, a ploy he knew that gave herself time to organize what she would say to him.

"I'm having a bit of a rough patch, Mikhail," she said almost briskly in a get-it-over with tone. She reached gracefully to claim a black mussel shell from those in the earth-colored pottery bowl. "I think you can help me—and Tanya. Most of all, Tanya."

"The girl you hold in the night? Your daughter?"

"My daughter," Ellie repeated softly. She looked into the flames and then down to the empty mussel shell; her fingers traced the smooth pearl and pink-colored interior as if feeling for answers that escaped her. "She has nightmares. Are you certain your parents know where to find me?"

"Of course. I am a thorough man and she will be well treated. My parents dote on children."

"Yes, I know." This time she spoke more thoughtfully, running her finger over the edge of the shell, testing its sharpness. "You're going to want everything, aren't you? Every detail."

There was no reason to soften his words with Ellie; she'd seen him in tough business deals, cutting right to the bottom line. "Of course."

Still watching the fire, Ellie drew her legs up on the chair, circling them with her arms. "Tanya isn't my natural child, but I love her as if she were. Hillary is her biological mother.''

Now everything made sense—Paul's reluctance to talk about his daughters, the telephone calls inquiring about Ellie, and Tanya's birth date, which ruled out Ellie as her biological mother.

Mikhail waited, sensing that Ellie was moving very carefully through her thoughts and words, as if she had replayed them many times before. Her voice sounded as if it came from an exhausted woman dragged through hell.

"Tanya is the family secret, Mikhail. Paul didn't want the scandal of Hillary's illegitimate child, or the possibility of social workers taking Tanya away from lack of care. You see, my half sister, whom I practically raised, lacks maternal instincts. Tanya was so adorable—she still is. Sweet, you know? I never could—'' Ellie's voice hitched as though holding back a sob. Then she swallowed, brushed her hand roughly across her eyes, and Mikhail waited for her to go on.

The flames crackled, firelight flickering on her face, catching her hair. "When Hillary couldn't be bothered with an infant, Paul hired a nurse to take care of Tanya.... My sister was off and running with her crowd as soon as she recovered her figure. And I was there, checking on this beautiful little unwanted baby left with a hired nurse who didn't care. Tanya was born just after the Amoteh's opening. I was there, too. There is something special about seeing a baby born—''

She smiled softly and now her eyes were dove gray. "She gurgled, you know. Happy little baby sounds...''

A slight sad frown slid over her expression. Ellie brush back her hair as though trying to focus on what she must do. "I fought with Hillary over her behavior, if you can call it that. Paul didn't bother to check what Hillary told him—and he didn't want to hear realities from me. He was fine with the situation as long as there was no bad publicity. Hillary's pregnancy was kept secret. She wasn't married and didn't know exactly who Tanya's father was. Paul still had plans to marry her off for business reasons. That's what his daughters are to him, you know—business assets.''

Ellie smiled slightly. ''Tanya was amazing, beautiful and I wanted her more than anything I'd wanted in my life. I wanted to adopt her. I chose to marry Mark, because I had this plan that two parents were better than one. He came from a good family. He wanted me—or rather he wanted a Lathrop heiress bred for the life he wanted—and I wanted Tanya. I was used to business deals, teethed on them, and marriage to Mark seemed sensible. I liked him. We were very compatible. We—we filled each other's needs. I wanted marriage, a home and the idea of a real family. I'm used to making trade-offs, Mikhail. I've made them all my life. I knew that I was exactly what Mark wanted, more of a business partner to make him look good. That was the master plan, to give Tanya a good home and a good father.''

She looked so weary and pale, and Mikhail's instincts were to tell her to rest. But he recognized that she had fought hard and now defeated, baring herself and her pride to him, that she needed to take these last steps by herself.

Ellie was quiet and then another blast of rain against the windows seemed to rouse her from her thoughts. ''Tanya was just six months old when I married Mark. We had talked about adoption prior to the wedding. He had agreed…and then he changed his mind. Someone had mentioned genetic defects to him, and he was afraid she'd— I spent the next six months trying to convince him that we needed to adopt Tanya. One of his ridiculous reasons not to adopt was that with Hillary's frequent changes in lovers, Tanya could have inherited any disease, he said. Basically, he wouldn't even bring up the subject to Paul. I did…I had to. My father can be…horrible. He believed that someday Hillary would marry and settle down and make a fine mother. So, I divorced Mark and adopted Tanya when she was two years old. Correction—I bought her from Hillary with everything I owned, and then I adopted Tanya legally. Tanya is my child—legally,'' Ellie repeated, clenching her fists until the knuckles glowed white beneath the skin.

To Mikhail, the thought that a woman could reject her own child was unthinkable—but then so was the fact that his ex-wife had an abortion rather than have their child. His child. The past bitterness went tearing through him again, unexpected and dark and hurting. He remembered his ex-wife's words. ''You chose the Amoteh and this godforsaken piece of sand. On those terms, I chose not to be a mother, not to be stuck in this wasteland. When we moved here, I thought it was only for a short time, that you needed to make your mark in the industry and then we would move to civilization. I simply changed my mind about having a baby, and that's that,'' JoAnna had said.

Mikhail pulled himself back from that stormy, primitive edge, that anger and sense of defeat—because his marriage was a failure and divorce the conclusion. To be truthful, perhaps he was as cold and boring as JoAnna had claimed. Perhaps he hadn't given her what a woman needed. Perhaps that was why his lovemaking had left her cold, why he felt empty and frustrated later.

He sorted through the years since he'd sent that crystal vase to Ellie as a wedding gift. With no word of Ellie's escapades, he'd thought that marriage had settled her. Paul had stopped speaking of his daughters. Meanwhile, she'd been divorced and had adopted her niece. ''And the problem? Why do you think you need me?''

When she looked at Mikhail, Ellie's eyes were filled with tears. Her hand trembled as she lifted it to dash them away. ''To Hillary, Tanya is just a…a thing to use. At first, Hillary hated her because childbirth had left stretch marks, and she'd lost her shape. I found Tanya, in her crib, alone at five months—though the nurse carefully locked the door before she went out with her friends. I vowed that would not happen again. Hillary was off somewhere, playing with another man, and she wasn't concerned at all. After that, I was around even more. I basically took Tanya to live with me, and Hillary didn't miss her at all.''

Mikhail remembered Hillary—wealthy, spoiled and willful, like Ellie. But there was a basic difference. Hillary acted and looked cheap. Paul actually paid her to stay away from business and social functions, but he wanted Ellie at his side to smooth any waves he created with his aggressive manners.

Except for the disaster of the botched real estate deal, Ellie was his little fix-it person—when she wanted. But if Paul and Ellie crossed swords, she was his personal disaster.

Mikhail did not want to share Paul's fate; he had already been cursed by one sharp-tongued, willful woman.

The woman curled in the huge chair was soft and vulnerable, and a mother fighting to protect her child. She turned to Mikhail, her eyes huge and sad. ''A year ago, Hillary said she wanted Tanya back to impress her new boyfriend. He thinks Hillary just had that one affair and excuses her for being too young to handle a Romeo type. He's wealthy and family-minded and Paul is delighted. He wants this marriage. He's obsessed by the idea of getting a Wall Street power broker into the family. This man's first wife wasn't fertile and he wants children—the complete family-man picture, you know…proving his manhood and healthy sperm count, and the family image for business, yada, yada, yada. He's ready to claim that Tanya is really his love child. Hillary and Paul will support him.''

Ellie shuddered and spoke quietly. ''I've used and sold everything I can to fight them legally—jewelry, stocks, wedding gifts, clothes—and six months ago, I started running. My father is a powerful man. He can make things…difficult. He sent men with Hillary to collect Tanya at the day care center—that's why she has nightmares of 'the big scary men' trying to take her away. Hillary came with them. She looks enough like me, and like Tanya, to pass as her 'aunt,' and that was when I knew we weren't

safe at all. I was working at an insurance office, and I left
as soon as the day care center called me to double-check
releasing Tanya without written permissions—and we
moved that night. Tanya still remembers that awful scene—
when Hillary is angry, she can be violent…abusive."

Ellie stood slowly as though she had come too far and
could go no farther. She stood in front of him with the air
of making a formal, desperate plea. "Mikhail, you are the
only man who can help us. Will you?"

Because he knew the players, Mikhail understood the
dynamics perfectly. Ellie was a fighter for causes she felt
deserved help, and he knew Hillary's selfishness and Paul's
determination to get his way, no matter who suffered. Now
a child was endangered—if Mikhail could trust Ellie to portray the situation correctly. From his experience, she knew
how to wrangle her way. "How do you see my part in this?
Why am I the only person who can help you?"

She smiled briefly, sadly, and stood like a warrior with
all her defenses shed. "Because you are the one man who
can match my father's power, and he respects you. In short,
I need an ally—someone to hold him off until I can get
back on my feet. I've picked you."

Mikhail tried not to notice the dark peaks of her nipples,
pressed against the white of his shirt. He stood abruptly,
and went to the window, considering the sleet and snow
with his hands thrust into his pockets. "You're asking me
to protect you and the child. Correct?"

Her voice was too soft over the crackling of the flames,
the howling of the wind, and the rain against the glass. And
yet, he heard her perfectly. "Only my daughter, Mikhail.
Do it for her."

"You realize what you're asking? Your father is not an
easy man."

"Neither are you. That is why you work so well together.
You're not his usual 'yes' man. He respects you for it. He
needs Tanya to portray the happy grandfather image to Hil-

lary's new man, to look like she's a perfect mother. She may play the part for a while, but when she's done, Tanya will be tossed aside. Don't let that happen, Mikhail.''

Mikhail remembered his last battle with Paul. The man was ruthless and in some cases unethical, and yet he was a shrewd businessman and carried no grudges when Mikhail proved him wrong. But a fight with Paul was always tough.

Ellie came to stand behind Mikhail. She gripped the back waistband of his slacks as though she was afraid he would escape her. ''I know exactly what I am asking. This resort means so much to you. You want to provide employment for the people you love in this town. They depend on the Amoteh's success. And to battle my father could endanger everything you've worked for.''

Mikhail nodded; Ellie's assessment was exact. ''I will want to meet the child…but I would rather not enter your family's fighting arena.''

''I know. I told her about you…that you were kind to children…that you knew wonderful stories and loved little girls. I told her that because I've seen you with children at the resort and campaign functions. Don't let my father and Hillary make Tanya into another emotional wreck, Mikhail.''

He could feel her body's warmth, the scent of it, clouding his decision to stay free of what she had asked. ''You're still tired. Go back to bed. We'll talk in the morning.''

Her hand left his slacks to grip his arm, her fingers slender and pale against his tanned skin. ''You'll think about helping Tanya?''

''One step at a time.''

''Yes, of course. I expected that much from you. You're very thorough in weighing your decisions.''

''Of course. We're done for now, Ellie. Make the most of this time and rest.''

With a long, tired sigh, she moved away from him and he missed her warmth. The rustle of the coverlet said she had slid into bed. But in the shadows, he felt her watching him, pleading with him to help.

She reminded him of a doe he'd once seen—soft, fearful, drained. He'd been camping, resting in the mountains, clearing his mind of business. Illegal hunters had used dogs to run down the animal, and exhausted, she'd settled into her deathly fate when Mikhail arrived to save her.

Saving Ellie was another matter. It endangered everything he'd worked for, the people who depended on him.

Only when he recognized her last sigh before sleep did he turn toward the woman on the bed.

He was a fool for even listening to her. Ellie Lathrop was a natural disaster to men, especially when she wanted her way—a true Kamakani curse. Perhaps Paul would listen to logic—but more than likely not, if Ellie had portrayed the situation realistically. Paul had always considered his daughters as bargaining chips in marriages that would bring him even more power and wealth. He wouldn't hesitate to use a child as a pawn.

Still, a child needed protection. Mikhail rubbed his hand across his jaw, and the sound of flesh against stubble matched his irritation. Above all, he wanted Ellie as a woman, and she would be a disaster.

Three

Ellie awoke the second time to a click of the big solid door. She lay quietly trying to pull herself from sleep into the harsh reality of Mikhail Stepanov…and the rejection he was certain to give her. Rest had brought the truth to her: *Mikhail was not likely to jeopardize the Amoteh.*

She caught his scent, felt him near, his presence almost pulsating around her, and her skin felt that prickle—like the hair of a cat sensing danger—just as it had last night. She didn't want to face him this morning, not when he had seen her stripped of pride, had seen her cry, and knew that she was practically penniless, with a child she couldn't support. Ellie had humbled herself to him, practically begged him. Tanya needed his protection, but on a more intimate level, Ellie resented being so helpless and dependent upon his decision.

And in her sleep, she had actually undressed in front of him, cuddled him as she would Tanya. Mikhail wasn't a

*man to cuddle; he was all taker, a man who moved me-
thodically to get his way.*

All pride fell beside the question. "I know you're there,
Mikhail. Will you help us?"

"*We* are here," he said quietly, warning her against any
further discussion about the child. "Tanya came to see
where you slept last night. She was worried about you."

Ellie opened her eyes to see Tanya, in her favorite blue
sweatsuit, seated on Mikhail's shoulders. He was dressed
in a black sweatshirt and worn jeans, still bearing the
night's stubble on his jaw.

In a business suit, he looked too intense, danger stream-
lined into quiet, groomed power. But dressed casually, the
sweatshirt stretching across his broad shoulders, he was raw
male.

Ellie trusted the man in the suit—the predictable, cold,
methodical man—not this relaxed one. His hair was rumpled by the child's hands that circled his forehead. But too
quiet, too watchful, Mikhail's sea-green eyes held Ellie's
as if warning her not to speak of the problem in front of
the child. Then that long slow prowl of his gaze down her
body, beneath the comforter, tugged at her senses, taking
away her breath.

She was still wearing his shirt, but she had just felt as
though those big hands had moved over her bare skin. His
eyes had glittered just that once, possessively, and the hair
on her nape rose. Whatever primitive and intimate thing it
was that sizzled in the air between them frightened and
warmed her.

A passing glance at a walnut-encased clock told her it
was eleven o'clock, and the late morning hour redefined
Mikhail's expression—he had always considered her
spoiled. "I was tired, okay?" she snapped at him.

"Evidently. Was the bed all right?" Mikhail's deep, sensual voice curled around her, reminding her that they had
shared the bed...that she had aroused him, that he had seen
her undress....

This time it was her turn to blush, her senses prickling as their eyes met and the quiet air sizzled between them.

And then she knew for certain that Mikhail wanted her now; not a sweet, loving need, but a raw passionate one to be filled and forgotten.

Ellie braced herself for another trade-off; she'd made a deal with one man that had failed, and if she had to—

Deep inside a warning voice told her that Mikhail wouldn't be easy to forget.

She breathed quietly, unsteadily, aware that her body had already reacted to him, her breasts tightening, that poignant clench in her lower stomach.

"Mama?" Tanya's uneven whisper said she needed reassurance, and Ellie instantly lifted up her arms.

Mikhail lowered Tanya to the bed and watched her slide into Ellie's waiting hug. As she always did, Ellie gave Tanya her full attention, soothing her fears. The girl cuddled close. "Good morning, pumpkin. Did you like that great big bed?" Ellie asked.

"I wasn't scared," Tanya whispered as her little hand smoothed Ellie's hair. "The man said you were very tired and needed to rest last night. You look all sort of rosy, Mommy. He was afraid if you came out in the rain, back to sleep with me, you would catch cold. And Fadey woke me up this morning. I think he likes me, just like a grandpa would. He showed me these pretty wooden eggs, all painted with people, and when you open one, guess what? There's another one inside."

"Of course," Mikhail said quietly, still watching Ellie, the tension of last night alive between them. *Would he help them?*

Ellie smoothed Tanya's blond silky hair and prayed that he would. "Have you made up your mind?" she asked quietly as, fascinated with the showroom, Tanya slid from the bed to wander around the room.

The answer cut through the shadowy air. "No. I have not."

"When?" Already, she was thinking of how she could manage to drive away from Amoteh. Because if Mikhail decided against helping her, he would probably tell Paul their whereabouts.

"When I have decided."

That arrogance grated; she had stripped away her pride, coming to him, asking for his help, and now he held her on tenterhooks, just as Paul would do. The men were too much alike, hard, impenetrable and looking for what a bargain could do for them.

And looking up at Mikhail from her vulnerable position in bed did little to soothe the nerves he had always scraped. Ellie clamped her lips against the words she wanted to let fly at him, and Mikhail's narrowed eyes said he had read her silent message.

He reached to push a button on the wall intercom. "Georgia? Would you come here, please? There is a little girl who wants to meet you. Perhaps she would like to see your kitchen and eat those croissants you've just made. And please put together a breakfast tray for two, please—a carafe of coffee? I'll be having breakfast in here with the girl's...mother."

"You could leave and give me a moment of privacy," Ellie whispered in a furious tone she didn't bother to disguise.

"No. You're the one asking, not me. I would advise you to be civilized and to wait until the child is out of hearing distance before you yell."

"Me? Civilized? Don't you dare—"

Mikhail's smile was brief and contained genuine humor, a notice that he had once more scored a hit. Then ignoring Ellie's frown, he walked to crouch beside Tanya, explaining the collection of shells in the pottery bowl.

Georgia, a plump woman wearing a white apron and a hairnet that crossed her forehead, arrived with the tray. Mikhail replaced the previous tray with the fresh one, and the scent of aromatic coffee and fresh croissants cruised the room.

In a heartbeat, Georgia had won Tanya's confidence, and they left the showroom, leaving Ellie alone with Mikhail. He poured two cups of coffee from the carafe and leaned against a tall dresser, watching her.

Watching her like a big predator, assessing, waiting. She could *feel* him trying to put her together, like a puzzle. Then there was something else in him, brooding and male and resentful.

That look pushed all her buttons, her anger leaping. He'd seen her without her pride, inferred her poverty by the hole in her briefs. Ellie sprung from the bed, tossing back the covers. "Tanya is not used to very many people, and I don't like you taking control of her. She gets frightened when she's away from me too long."

"And you resent that she isn't in *your* control, dependent upon you. She isn't a baby. She's a young child with a natural need to have playmates other than you."

That Tanya could be swayed so easily did bother Ellie. She walked to the tray and took the coffee cup he offered, splashed with the Amoteh's strawberry logo. "I know she needs playmates. But we haven't had time to settle in before they found us and we had to move again."

"You're angry with me. Why?"

Because he looked too rugged, as if he could withstand any fight, and because— "Do you think I actually like asking you for help? You're determined to make me squirm, before you turn me down. Oh, I know the routine. Paul likes to play that game."

She was shaking with anger, the scenes with her father too familiar. He would ask all the questions, make her answer, and then, when he was tired, he refused her needs. The whole process had served to humiliate her, even as a child. Emotional baggage? Yes, but she couldn't allow that treatment again.

Ellie placed the coffee cup down on the tray with a click,

careless of the spillage. "Look. It was a mistake to ask you for anything. Now leave. I'm getting dressed and we're getting out of here."

Mikhail placed his coffee cup aside slowly, thoughtfully. "You haven't answered all my questions."

"No, and I'm not going to. If you're not leaving, then I am." With that, she walked to where she had shed her clothing. She frowned as she picked it up, remembering that Mikhail had seen her undress. She'd been so vulnerable with one man, and she wasn't—

She had one hand on the doorknob when Mikhail picked her up. Surprised, she didn't have time to fight before he tossed her on the bed. "Stay put."

No one, not even her father, had ever manhandled her. Ellie pushed upward, only to find Mikhail's hand on her forehead, pushing her back down. Frustrated and worried and tired, she'd come too far—Ellie struck out blindly, but Mikhail was too quick for her.

In a flurry of movement and cloth, he had cocooned her in the comforter, making movement impossible. She thrashed within the tight clasp of the cloth and finally, winded, spoke furiously, quietly. "If I could just get my hands on you..."

"If looks could kill," he murmured as she tossed her head and blew a strand of hair from her face.

He sat beside her on the bed, controlling her too easily— physically controlling her where Paul had once used other methods with a young Ellie. "Let me go, Mikhail."

But those dark green eyes, as brooding as the ocean on a stormy day, were searching her face, touching her too intimately. His gaze darkened, locking on her lips, tracing them. She couldn't breathe, feeling exposed with Mikhail too close and too powerful, and she resented the blush creeping up her cheeks. In her adult lifetime, she'd learned to protect herself, never letting anyone truly see into her. And now, she could feel Mikhail probing, taking her apart, appraising the pieces too thoroughly....

"Stop watching me."

"Stop ordering me."

He was breathing too quietly, intent upon her as he looked slowly down, then up her body. There was just that tensing of his jaw, the slight flare of his nostrils and the sense that he was too intimately dangerous to her.

"Is your ex-husband going to be a problem in this?" he asked quietly, searching her face, and again that tracing of her mouth, a sensual touch that shivered and warmed in the air between them.

"Mark thinks Tanya should go back to Hillary. No, he won't be a problem. He's remarried and has a child. He has the wife he wants." She didn't know why she whispered, only that the spacious showroom now seemed as intimate as a bedroom.

"Did that hurt you? That he would have a child with another woman?"

She blinked, trying to making the connection. "No.... Why?"

"If you loved him, it might hurt. Did you love him?"

She didn't want Mikhail prowling too close to her emotions. Love wasn't discussed in her family. "That's got nothing to do with it."

"I want to know how the players stand in this game. You practically raised Hillary, from what I understand. And now you have her child."

"*My* child, Mikhail. Tanya is my child," Ellie stated fiercely. "Are you going to call Paul?"

She sensed he was satisfied, if only a little as he spoke. "Not now. I want to know more. If you are playing a game with her to defy your family—"

"How can you say that? You know them."

"Of course. For now, you and Tanya will stay with my parents—they've already asked."

"You won't call Paul just yet?"

"No."

She could have kissed him. She badly needed rest and

thinking room, and Tanya needed even more—she needed the security of a home that the Stepanov family could provide, if only for a time.

She eased a hand up to press it against his cheek. She must have shown her gratitude, because Mikhail frowned slightly, then a slow warmth began to rise up his cheeks. She could feel it dance and pulse beneath her fingertips.

Mikhail's hand curled around her wrist and removed it slowly, firmly. "I'll want the list of places you've lived in the last six months."

Business, she thought. Mikhail was good at details, but she had nothing to hide now. "I understand. You need confirmation."

"Of course." He stood abruptly, nodded and left the room.

Ellie lay on the bed, easing from the tight cloth, and tried to pinpoint Mikhail's unsettling expression.

As she dressed to join Tanya in the kitchen, Ellie decided that he was embarrassed by her gratitude. She had reached inside him to where a human heart lurked.

She hummed a bit and served herself a buttery croissant, slathered with the Amoteh's house strawberry jam. For the moment, she had sanctuary for Tanya. On a more personal and separate level, she had Mikhail in retreat, a possibility she couldn't imagine. He'd actually blushed. All her taunting and playing had failed, and now, without trying, she'd scored a hit on Mikhail—she'd seen just that sliver inside him, the real man. The stakes now were too big to revel in the game or her win. Tanya had to be safe and Mikhail—

Well, Mikhail was Mikhail. Ellie didn't understand him at all, but she knew she could trust him—on one level. He had said he wouldn't call Paul, and that meant he wouldn't.

With that, she inhaled the scent of lemon furniture polish as if it were fresh hope and slid a paper tablet from a lamp table. She began listing the places she'd lived with Tanya in the last six months. There were so many, and always, sooner or later, Hillary or Paul's emissaries would arrive....

*   *   *

In the gray of early morning, with the fog curling around the tourist pier, the shops deserted now, Mikhail thought about the woman sleeping in his parents' home. She had been too soft and warm from sleep this morning, cuddling Tanya beside her, the two looking so much alike, gray eyes and blond hair, almost mother and child.

He'd wanted her. The idea shocked and repelled him. Mikhail knew what she was—spoiled, and a user; she had admitted to contriving her marriage to get the child.

Yet the affection between Ellie and Tanya couldn't be dismissed, not the smoothing of her hands on the child's hair, the kiss on her rosy cheek, the snuggling against her, as if the girl gave her comfort. Children often comforted, just by being near and sweet.

Thoughts of Ellie pushed against him as unrelentingly as the ocean waves rolled against the pier.

Seagulls gleamed ghostly white in the fog, settling in to watch the man prowling the pier. In the off-season, he was alone.

Mikhail inhaled the salty, frigid air and scanned the fog sliding along the shoreline. He'd grown up here, wild and free, digging for razor clams with Jarek, netting Dungeness crabs and selling them.

Other than the few Stepanov furniture workers, the employment opportunities had been slight in the small ocean-side community then, but now, the Amoteh Resort brought tourists and work. Trinny, a bold, big woman with a brood of growing children, was even now placing the Amoteh's strawberry logo on cups to be used in the resort and sold in the gift shop. In the summer, the pier's shops would be filled with tourist goods, keepsakes to remind them of their visit. The air would smell of excitement, salt and clam chowder; the sounds of vacationing families mixing with that of the townspeople running the shops.

Ed and Bliss, Jarek's in-laws, would be happy hawking worry stones and tie-dyed T-shirts.

And by summer, Leigh, his wife, would be showing off the baby to be born next month. Leigh was round and glowing, and both fearful and happy. Jarek watched her every move. According to their mother, Stepanov men were excellent "hoverers" and spoiled their wives without caution.

Mikhail would never know how it felt to hover and spoil a pregnant wife. He fought the clench of bitterness that his own child had been destroyed before its first breath. He wondered when that emptiness would leave. The need to have children and a home ran deep in the traditional Stepanov males, and Mikhail had used the resort to fill that need.

He shrugged slightly within his peacoat and tugged the collar higher against the damp cold. He had what he wanted—the success of the Amoteh.

If he protected Ellie and Tanya, gave them shelter, he could lose everything he'd worked for, endangering the resort and the people he loved.

The boards creaked beneath his feet; an icicle broke free from a shop, shattering on the ice and snow that would quickly melt with the warmth predicted for the day. The fog stirred, and out of it came a man as tall and powerfully built as Mikhail. "Jarek."

The brothers stood together as men, bound by blood and boyhood, watching the day light, skimming the shore, the seagulls already searching for fresh food on the shoreline.

"Dinner at the folks' was good last night," Jarek said quietly.

"Um." Mikhail sensed his younger brother picking through words, and he sensed that at the end of the trail there would be Ellie.

"Stroganoff. Lots of cookies…those little gingersnaps filled with raspberry jam that Dad likes. Apparently Tanya and Mom have a baking thing going. Ellie was too quiet. She's waiting for something, and at each sound she looked toward the door, as if expecting the only missing member of our family—you. She's tired and afraid, too afraid, as if she's run on nerves for a long time. She never let that show to the girl, though. From her clothes and that car, I'd say she's down on her luck. The heiress of the Lathrop fortune, down on her luck. Makes you wonder why she's here, doesn't it?''

Mikhail sighed. His family wanted to know why he'd missed his favorite meal. The chosen emissary was Jarek.

"She's a disaster, you know. She has been since I met her in Paul's Seattle office almost eleven years ago. About five years ago, she fouled a big business deal for Mignon International. They were set to buy a high-priced piece of land for a resort near Cannes. The contract had been negotiated and renegotiated. Ellie knew the terms and Paul's plans to build on the part of the property he needed, split the rest and sell it off at premium prices. The seller decided to split it himself and squashed the deal. If Ellie's around, there is trouble.''

Jarek's shoulder nudged Mikhail's. "You're brooding, so she's evidently troubling you, big brother. She stayed in the showroom last night. Georgia said you'd fixed a tray for her that evening, and ordered one this morning. There were two cups used.''

"Georgia talks too much.''

"Uh-huh. And you're afraid Ellie will run. Before coming here, you stopped at the house just long enough to lift the hood of her car. I'd say it's not going anywhere for a while. Could it be that she's got your motor revved?''

"Not a chance,'' Mikhail lied to avoid his younger brother's teasing. Younger brothers had a way of taunting and paying back. "Lay off. How's Leigh?'' Mikhail asked to waylay Jarek and the knowing grin spreading across his face.

The grin turned into a soft woozy smile of an expectant father. "Cute. Beautiful. More than beautiful. I love her. She is my life,'' Jarek finished simply and looked out over the tide frothing nearby and across the ocean's black swells as if longing for her.

He held up a sack with the Amoteh's logo and the grin widened. "Leigh's favorite breakfast—strawberry jam and sardines and buttermilk. I had to raid Georgia's pantry. We're out and we're having breakfast at the folks' this morning. I'm holding out for Mom's blueberry pancakes."

In the other direction loomed the narrow passage of water necessary to reach Strawberry Hill, a peninsula jutting out into the Pacific. When the tide was up, Deadman's Rock marked the passage and Strawberry Hill could only be reached by boat, or the curving roundabout road by land.

Jarek's brief look toward Deadman's Rock said he remembered his first wife, who believed in the curse, and who had died, in love with the chieftain. Yet Leigh had traveled the same stretch of water, and Deadman's Rock had not taken her life. She had danced before Kamakani's grave, a woman who knew her own heart and who would protect those she loved.

"Ellie wants my help. If I give it, I'll endanger the Amoteh," Mikhail said quietly, wanting his brother to know why he brooded. "Paul won't be happy."

Jarek nodded. "You'll do what you think is right. You always have. She's chosen you because you're a match for Paul."

"Yes. But she's trouble. I've seen her in action."

"She trusts you. You are a man to trust. And she disturbs you. I've seen it before, at the opening of the Amoteh. She sets you off and you her. I was enjoying flirting with her, but you were in her sights. Ellie wanted to take you down. She's not like JoAnna, Mikhail. She's got a heart and she's a natural mother. Her entire world is that little girl."

Mikhail shook his head. "There's too much at stake. But I'm thinking."

He was thinking about Ellie, about touching her and taking her to fill the sharp need within him now.

It was only a need, Mikhail thought as Jarek nodded and moved silently off into the fog, eager to return to his wife.

The tide frothed and ebbed against the sand as Mikhail

stood locked in his thoughts. Then a slender figure delicately picked its way around the driftwood logs, down to the shore and he found himself moving toward Ellie and trouble.

"Ellie." Her name was a flat statement on Mikhail's lips, not a greeting, as if she were on his problem list and had to be solved. Even before he spoke, she'd known he was near—her body had tensed, the hair on her nape rising. She shivered within her light jacket, the hood up over her hair.

Chilled in her damp jeans and canvas shoes, she kept her gaze locked on the dark swells, the white line of foam marking the bridge between water and land, the seagulls hunting for food, sandpipers scurrying here and there. Clumps of seaweed on the beach almost seemed alive and moving as the water slid through them.

The sound of the waves and the fog marked an eerie time, a lonely one, and a reckoning with a hope that couldn't be reality. Mikhail wasn't likely to endanger everything he had worked for, or the income of people depending on them. Last evening at the Stepanovs, she understood how vital the community had become, lives affected by Mikhail's resort, the tourists it brought.

She'd been crying in the lonely hour, letting her fears envelop her. She didn't want him to see her weakness; she'd exposed enough of herself already. He was enough like Paul to move in to pick over the pieces and find the most tender, raw ache of a loving parent. *She couldn't provide for her child.*

Ellie could feel Mikhail behind her, the warmth of his body, the intimacy of the fog wrapping around them. "We can't stay here. I have to find work, and I won't be responsible for keeping you from your family by staying there. Whatever you might think of me, I don't live off other people. I paid my dues with Paul. I practically raised Hillary for him, and I didn't do a very good job. And so help me, I still love her and I'm fighting to keep Tanya from being messed up like my sister and myself. So I'm not feeling up to you this morning, Mikhail."

"Shut up." The command was unexpected, fierce.

She turned on him, hands clenched into fists. "You're so like him."

"Am I?" His answer was too quiet, so quiet, she could hear water drip from a stack of driftwood...plop, plop...

This morning, in the intimate dawn, he was even taller and more ominous than in his resort. A muscle clenched in his jaw, covered by stubble. His usually well groomed hair was waving, beaded with mist. His eyes were narrowed, dark gleaming pinpoints that burned her face, looked inside her fears and tore them out of her....

"I have to get work, Mikhail," she said unsteadily. "I'm going to wire a friend for money—just enough to get us out of here. All I'm asking is two or three days in which you don't call Paul."

He was silent and she frowned. "I'm sorry that I'm too tired and on edge and that I can't give Tanya what she needs, a wonderful home like your parents', or like Jarek and Leigh's. Not just now. But I will. I thought about it, and it just won't work here. Hillary is one thing and Paul another, and together they are cruel, selfish people. I can't risk what they could do to Tanya if you turned us in."

Mikhail's dark look took in her hunched shoulders and ripped down her body, heating it oddly, and then back up to her face. "You're shivering and you're wet."

She laughed unsteadily, resenting the panic that had slipped through her. "Life has been hectic for the last six months. I had to have time to think this morning, Mikhail. Alone. You're in my personal space, buddy. Shove off."

"It's a public beach, and not all that crowded either," he said slowly, studying her.

He was standing too close and whatever pulsed hot and alive between them hitched up a notch until it burned Ellie's skin and her senses tingled. "*You're* crowding me."

"There's always that between us, isn't there?" he asked quietly as if to himself.

"I don't know what you mean."

But she knew exactly. If Mikhail was within striking distance, she had to tear at him, taunt him, anything to shake through that control. "If you weren't so afraid—"

Now the fog seemed to stop moving, and the world stilled around them. "Of what am I afraid?" he asked very slowly.

The need to lash out at him was too strong. Right now, she was on edge and frightened for Tanya, and regretting that she had stripped her pride for a man who wasn't likely to help her. Ellie ripped off her jacket's hood and lifted her face to the damp mist. She didn't want to let him into her inner thoughts, especially concerning him. "Forget it."

"I am not afraid of Paul."

"I know. You're a match for him. He admires you. That's why I thought—"

The mist seemed to hover, still and alert between them as Mikhail spoke quietly, "Then, of what am I afraid?"

What did anything matter now that she had bared her fears to him and had asked him for help? She might as well serve him a reality check—her opinion of him as a sensitive man. "Look. Your love life is no concern of mine. I haven't got time or energy for your problems. But here it is—you got married, you got hurt and now you've wrapped yourself up in that resort so you'll never be touched by life—and love. Oh, you love your family, of course, but you've sworn off women. You're afraid to get involved. Anyone can see that."

"Can they?" Mikhail asked darkly, studying her with that close, burning intensity that seemed to make the sand shiver beneath her sodden shoes. The waves seemed to slow and stop, the fog still and intimate, and Ellie could only hear the sound of her quickening heartbeat.

Then with a rough, reluctant sigh, he tugged her to him

and took her mouth with enough heat to make her forget everything but taking as he was taking....

Mikhail's lips were hard and open and savage and claiming and hot, so hot and fierce and possessive that Ellie arched up to meet him. Everything that she had sensed hidden beneath Mikhail's sleek cold exterior was just beneath the surface, hot and real, and it was hers at last. She knew exactly why she had to fight him, to taunt him, to find this man, raw and true and strong within her arms. His passion was enough to burn away everything else.

He was just what she needed, as strong as she was, as fierce in his dark mood, the balance she needed to anchor her. He was big and hard and real and hungry.

Ellie sank into the hunger, the taste, the wild, free need to meet Mikhail, to capture him, to devour him—no gentle, sweet claiming, but a primitive reality of needs and heat. She pushed him away slightly, an instinctive feminine test to see how much the male desired, how much he would take in the game, the hunger, and Mikhail brought her closer.

Mikhail held her tight, just as she wanted, locked against him.

She found his hair with her fingers, gripping hard to hold him, to keep what she wanted close and hers.

Mikhail slanted his kiss, taking it deeper, one hand cupping her head, the other open and possessive on her body. The kiss was glorious, wild and free and strong. It was as if she were being devoured and returning the favor, as if the lid had been torn free from everything she wanted and all she had to do was take and take.

His breath was rough and uneven against her skin, but the amazing heat—

Mikhail's hand slid up her body, found her breast beneath the light cloth and then his coat was open and she was inside, pressed hard against him, her arms around his waist, her hands reveling in that taut powerful back, clawing at the cloth, wanting the flesh beneath.

"So now it has begun," he whispered roughly amid other bitter, rushing words she didn't understand.

She sensed him easing away, and in the aftermath of the storm could only weakly seek shelter close to him, her face against the warmth of his throat. Instinctively, she bit him lightly, partly because she wanted him to remember this moment, and because she wanted to mark him as her own. She wanted to tear away the woman who had hurt him deeply and yet she had to protect herself, because Mikhail was not an easy man. "Nothing has begun. If you think you can scare me with that, think again."

She could feel his smile against her cheek. And this time, his kiss came more gently, seeking, asking....

Four

Fadey opened the door to the Stepanov home and grinned widely at Mikhail's scowl and the squirming, furious woman dressed in his peacoat.

"Here, take her," Mikhail said roughly as he entered the house. He tossed Ellie into Fadey's arms and walked toward the kitchen. His mother's kitchen had always soothed storms, with its blend of solid wood Stepanov cabinets and Texas influence. Right now, Ellie's temper matched the string of red chili peppers beside his mother's stove, and his own mood was not far behind.

Mikhail had instinctively wanted to bring her to his parents. That need shocked him, because Jarek had carried Leigh to the Stepanov's home in just the same way—as if he'd found the woman whom he intended to keep.

Keeping Ellie… He was asking for disaster, Mikhail brooded, and yet the feel of her in his arms had created an ache for more.

Fadey grinned widely and tossed Ellie back into Mikhail's arms. "No, you take her back. I already have a woman."

"Augh!" Mikhail found himself snarling.

"How…dare…you…." Ellie was hissing, pushing against his shoulders with her hands.

He wanted to take her to bed—his bed. He wanted to finish what had begun on the beach…he wanted to taste and take and possess and be possessed, because now with her twisting in his arms, he knew that Ellie was his match…his match, his woman…he wanted to—

He denied that thought and tossed her back to Fadey, who was chuckling.

Mikhail turned toward the kitchen again and away from the raging need to sweep Ellie back into his arms. On the beach, he'd wanted to claim her fully, to possess her. The sensual purrs deep in her throat had ignited his senses, his need to caress that long curved body with his hands, to hold her as she quivered, taut against him. He could still feel that storm of silky hair in his hands, the smooth heat of her skin against his face, the rapid pulse in her throat.

She'd responded too honestly for a game and that was unnerving; he'd tasted the sweetness of her open lips, felt her heat rise and—

He stiffened at his father's chuckle behind him and Ellie's "Let me go. Let me at him. He's just showing off that he's bigger and stronger than I am. But I'm a whole lot smarter. I can take him down anytime."

Mikhail stopped and turned slowly to see Fadey laughing and restraining Ellie by an arm around her waist. If Mikhail touched her now, felt that slender curved body arching up to him, he'd—

"I kissed her. She liked it, and now she's mad. I had to carry her here, otherwise she would have run from me and I would have had to chase her. I would have kissed her again, and she would have liked it, and then been more mad. It made everything much simpler to carry her," Mikhail stated baldly. "She wants me, of course."

"Of course," Fadey agreed, his grin widening.

Ellie glared at him, her eyes the color of storm clouds, her lips trembling with unspoken words. Furious, she seemed to shoot off sparks, her hair gleaming and alive as she trembled, her body taut. She shook loose from Fadey's arm and stood with her legs braced apart, her fists balled at her side. Clearly fighting to restrain herself, Ellie blew back a stand of hair from her forehead. "I'm going to take you down, bud. Your son is too arrogant, Fadey."

She was glorious, Mikhail thought. His body heated and hummed, the need to feel her lips burn his warring with his cautions....

He sensed that if caution and layers of civilization were torn away, she could devour him sensually, as he could her— In effect, Ellie was a dangerous, exciting, emotional woman who would always test him, verbally or sensually.

Those kisses on the beach had shown more passion and tender excitement than intimacy with his ex-wife, and now that he'd had a taste he hungered for more. The stark need to fit her body to his, without the restrictions of clothing, to run his hands over those curves, to taste her, riveted him as they stared at each other.

From across the room, he could feel her passion—and her shimmering fury, like a high ocean storm enveloping him.

Ellie jolted him back to his body's hunger, whether he liked it or not.

Retreat? Yes, but then he would never know how it would feel to claim her, to take and be taken, because Ellie would be a fierce, wild lover—or more devastatingly, a sweet, tender one. And he had to follow the path set on the beach....

"I apologize for Mikhail. I am afraid he is a little like his brother and his father," Fadey said when he stopped chuckling. Then to Mikhail, he said quietly, "So it has begun. The storm and the woman."

Mikhail inhaled roughly. He nodded curtly, admitting the

truth his father had recognized instantly. "She isn't what I want."

Fadey shrugged lightly, an acceptance that life brought as it chose.

"If you think I would actually want someone like him," Ellie shot back, as her hair shimmered and glowed, almost alive around her face. "Think again. He—he picked me up and carried me. He was just showing that he's the superior male, he's stronger, that he…"

"You want me, and you know it," Mikhail stated, because there was nothing to hide from his father now. Ellie bore the look of a woman who had been well kissed, and for whatever perversity lurked in Mikhail now, he was pleased that she bore his touch.

He wasn't a possessive man, or an emotional, passionate one, and now he didn't understand himself. How perfectly Ellie.

"I would not have you served on a platter!" Ellie's furious retort followed Mikhail into his mother's kitchen.

Locked in his frustrating desire for Ellie and the past moment of fighting, carrying her to his parents' home, while he heard exactly how she was going to bring him down, he wasn't prepared for the scene that met him. The sprawling dinner table was filled with family and Leigh's parents, Bliss and Ed. Mary Jo's blueberry pancakes were on the plates and seated on Jarek's lap, Tanya was all soft little girl, dressed in her blue-striped flannel pajamas and clutching her doll.

Mikhail stood still, trapped by the knowledge that his family had probably heard everything. He struggled for an explanation and decided there was none; silence was his best defense; they had heard him complain about Ellie often enough. *I would not have you served on a platter!*

The silence swelled and pressed and finally Mikhail felt obliged to say, "I have not seen platters big enough to accommodate me. Therefore, that is not possible."

Jarek exploded in laughter. "Then we'd better make one."

Fadey came behind Mikhail, and hugged him roughly, playfully. "So now the family is together. Ellie will be here in a minute. She is—ah, refreshing herself."

Mikhail fought the impulse to go to Ellie, to hold her once more against him, to feel her breath on his cheek. He reached down for Tanya, who had squirmed down to run to him. She squealed as Mikhail hefted her into the air and then enclosed her with a warm hug and a nuzzle. She leaned back in his arms, her gray eyes wide and serious, as she patted his cheek with her small hand. Mikhail's frustration with himself and Ellie instantly turned to so much petals in the wind. Ellie was right; this little girl needed to be protected from Hillary and Paul's coldness. She shouldn't be used as a pawn.

When he placed Tanya on her feet, she ran to Fadey, whose laughter ricocheted around the Mexican tile and brown glazed pots in the spacious kitchen. Fadey eased into a big Stepanov chair with the girl on his lap. "Feed me, woman," he ordered his wife with a big grin.

"Now, darlin'," Mary Jo said easily in her Texas drawl as she added another two plates to the breakfast table. A leggy former beauty queen, she wore a cotton shirt tucked into light denim jeans, her blond and gray chignon perfectly elegant and in place. She stood on tiptoe to kiss her son's cheek. There was just that narrowing of her eyes that warned him not to let his dark mood spoil a family breakfast.

Then her smile said she understood; she knew that any time Ellie was mentioned or in the vicinity, Mikhail usually had reason to brood. "There's the pancakes, Fadey, and you've been feeding yourself for years. Sit down, Mikhail. You're just in time."

Mikhail was sensually on edge, badly needing to complete the sizzling kiss with Ellie. He scowled at Jarek's big grin.

"Ohhh," Bliss crooned sympathetically and rose from the table. Bliss and Ed were overage flower children, loving and gentle, and settling in for their first grandchild. Bliss was particularly astute about feelings—"auras," she called them—and Mikhail could feel her prowling around his mood as she came to study him, patting his cheek gently. "You're bristling, Mikhail. Goodness, I can just feel those hot little vibes spearing from you. You're upset, and—"

Bliss frowned slightly. "Dear, it is more than upset. You're positively humming with something else that has just been brought to the surface somehow. My goodness—"

Just then Ellie breezed into the kitchen, shot him a furious look and started to walk around him, her head held high. "Good morning, everyone. This smells delicious."

Already sensitized, Mikhail's body responded to her immediately. Only a man who had kissed her thoroughly, wrapped her against him and breathed the scent of her body would feel pleasure in the slight swell of her lips, the flush of her cheeks, the flashing heat of her eyes.

He couldn't resist a downward look at her body, curved within her red chunky sweater and worn jeans. Almost unnoticeable, the peaks of her breasts were still hardened, and it gave him immense pleasure to know that she reacted as he had, that she still carried that passion within her, not easily forgotten.

They were in tune with each other, at least physically. The rest would be open warfare.

Bliss slowly studied Ellie and then turned to Mikhail, and he groaned inwardly. Under Bliss's inspection, he felt like a sulky little boy, and he knew what to expect.

"Group hug," Bliss said softly but firmly as she wrapped one arm around Mikhail and the other around Ellie. Each refused to budge, to come closer. Ellie stared furiously at Mikhail. He grimly returned the favor.

Bliss's gaze went from one to another. "Goodness. She's just absolutely quivering. Can you feel it, Mikhail?"

Mikhail banked the groan inside him. He'd felt Ellie quiver, all right, hot and sweet and hungry. And in the Stepanov home, there were few secrets, especially with Bliss's "vibration" and "aura" revelations.

"Let's just get this over with," he stated grimly. He was a veteran of Bliss's group hugs to solve arguments.

"What if I don't want to?" Ellie taunted, and stepped back to fold her arms over her chest.

Bliss looked sympathetically at her. "Now, dear. You know it isn't good to—"

Mikhail reached past Bliss, tugged Ellie into his arms and kissed her. Surprised, she came sweetly against him, and he luxuriated in the softness he wanted, the scent. When he heard a purr deep in her throat that shot heat into his blood, he struggled for control. He set her back from him, a bit roughly, because his fingers wanted to dig in and take.

She looked up at him blankly, her mouth slightly parted as her hands latched onto the countertop behind her. She looked flushed and sweet and stunned and— "There," Mikhail said quietly, disturbed by the gentleness within him, the need to comfort her. "I guess that about says it. Let's eat."

"'About says it. Let's eat,'" Ellie repeated as though in a trance as he eased her into a chair beside his at the table.

"She's cute like that, don't you think?" Mikhail asked Jarek, who was grinning, though his wife's nudging elbow had just reminded him of his manners.

"Now, Precious," Jarek said to tease his wife, formerly known as Bliss and Ed's "Precious Blossom." When Leigh opened her mouth to protest the nickname, Jarek kissed her. "Mother of my child, my love and my life," he said softly.

Leigh reacted with a delighted blush, her coppery curls dancing. "Keep looking at me like that, big boy, and I'll let you share my sardines," she offered.

"Mmm. You can have my share," Jarek returned with a grin.

"Now, Ellie-darlin'," Mary Jo soothed in her drawl. "Don't think too badly of my boys, will you? It's their father's influence, not mine. In Texas, we're a lot calmer and we get there just the same. And, Mikhail, you mind your manners."

Mikhail was thirty-nine, a successful businessman, and still his mother could make him feel as if he were ten.

Fadey looked as blissful as an expectant grandfather could be, and Mikhail suspected even greater expectations in that intent look crossing from Mikhail to Ellie. If there was one thing Fadey and Mary Jo dreamed of in their rich life, it was for a houseful of grandchildren. "It's not going to happen," Mikhail said quietly to his father.

"We'll see. A new broom sweeps—"

"Fadey..." Mary Jo warned, because Mikhail wasn't a man to push.

As Mikhail began to enjoy his mother's famous pancakes, he could feel Ellie thinking, tick-tock. She ate slowly, methodically, and then, as if sensing her mother was upset, Tanya came to sit on her lap. "You kissed my mommy," she accused Mikhail, frowning at him. "Why?"

"It's a thing people do when they like each other," Mikhail said gently.

"A man tried to kiss her once like that, and she hit him and made him go away. He didn't like me and she said she didn't like him anymore, but they were married once. He wanted her, but not me, and she said it was 'a package deal.' She said I was more important than anyone like him."

"But I like you." Mikhail bent slightly to kiss the little girl, who obviously needed reassurance. When he offered his arms, Tanya came into them, snuggling sweetly against him and sitting on his lap.

With her little body cuddled against him, Mikhail knew that he would do his best to protect her from Hillary and Paul. In Ellie's place, he would have done the same thing.

"Here," Tanya said, offering her doll, which he cradled in his other arm.

Over Tanya's head, Mikhail met Ellie's soft gray eyes. Sadness lurked there, and fear that tore at Mikhail's heart. He couldn't bear to see her fight alone, and he knew the cold, cruel and treacherous dangers of Paul and Hillary.

"So are you coming to work for me or not?" he asked gently as he slid a finger through Ellie's hair, wrapping the silky length around his finger and studying the naturally sun-lightened shades.

He saw no reason to hide his fascination with her from his family. The Stepanovs did not keep secrets, they freely shared their moods and feelings with each other.

"Absolutely not. You're a disaster."

Her snit delighted him—they both knew that kiss had changed the war to a different level, a sensual one, tit-for-tat, hunger meeting hunger. "Think about it."

She arched an eyebrow. "And did you check out my references?" she asked tauntingly, referring to the list of places she and Tanya had lived in the last six months.

"Of course." It was a sad trail, from small cabins to motels, from one job to another, and Mikhail realized how much it had cost Ellie to finally come to him.

She turned to look at the pancakes Fadey had placed in her plate, slathering them with butter. Fadey patted her shoulder. "Eat. Mikhail has offered you a job. You have a warm home for your child and good food. We are family. We laugh, we love. How much better can life be?"

Ellie did not look up, and her hand shook slightly as she lifted her fork. "I'll think about it."

A child needing reassurance when her parent was troubled, Tanya eased into Ellie's arms. She cuddled the little girl close, kissing her hair, and Tanya's small hand stroked Ellie's face. "What's wrong, Mama? Don't you like it here? You get that sad look when we have to leave."

Ellie kissed Tanya's hand and rocked her. "You'd like to stay, wouldn't you, pumpkin?"

"I want to be with you," Tanya stated firmly, and pressed her face against Ellie's throat, her arms tight in a hug.

"Always," Ellie whispered adamantly, her voice uneven.

Mikhail couldn't resist smoothing Ellie's shoulders, comforting her. She had fought alone long enough.

A man deeply touched and his emotions visible, Fadey sniffed just once and roughly wiped his eyes with his napkin. "This little girl says she doesn't know her grandpa. While I am sure he is a fine man, I would like to be her grandpa, too. What do you think, eh, little one? I need some little girls to sit on my lap and to hug. Poor Fadey. Grandpa Fadey, eh? That is what you call me, eh, Tanya?" he asked cheerfully.

Clearly excited, Tanya remained where she was, looking at Ellie, who nodded. With a whoop, the little girl squirmed out of her lap and ran to Fadey's open arms. "Grandpa Fadey!"

"Hey. And Grandma Mary Jo, of course."

"Of course," Tanya said with Stepanov-like arrogance. She beamed when Mary Jo bent to kiss her lips. "Grandma." The word slid out easily as a child's wish come true. "Grandma," Tanya repeated.

Ellie's indrawn breath, her soft expression, that quiver of her lips, said she was deeply grateful. "Thank you," she whispered, because a child needed safety and to belong to a family.

Across Tanya's blond curls, Fadey met Ellie's eyes. "You stay, little one. Mikhail is a good man, and so is Jarek. My two good sons, so different, so much the same. You are home now. If you go, you will always have this home."

Mikhail brushed the tear from Ellie's cheek. Clearly deeply touched, she bent her head, her face hidden by her hair. She was unused to the open warmth of the Stepanov home. "Mikhail, help me," she whispered as a second tear, silver and shining dropped in the morning sunlight.

"Of course. A hug, right, Bliss?"

"Most definitely."

In typical Fadey style, Mikhail reached to surround Ellie with his arms, giving her a big playful bear hug, waggling her a little before releasing her into her chair.

When she tensed and those eyes shot thunderbolts at him, he grinned and kissed her on both cheeks, Fadey-style. "It's just a custom. Don't get all worked up over it, Ellie."

"You couldn't work me up if you tried."

"No?" he drawled, his body humming.

On her way to the stove, Mary Jo slapped the top of his head. "Hey. Behave. You're not that grown-up, Mikie," Mary Jo reminded him.

While Mikhail sulked over the use of a childhood nickname that he preferred would be forgotten, Ellie smirked beautifully. "Mikie," she repeated.

Mikhail knew she would use his nickname to torture him. "No."

"Yes, Mikie," she cooed and batted her lashes at him.

Mikhail decided to retreat from the battlefield and grimly ate his pancakes.

Mikhail ignored the morning's cold slashing rain, because he needed it to clear his head. He tore away a wind battered stand of dry grass on his way up to Chief Kamakani's grave. In summer, the fields on either side of the rocky trail leading to the summit would be lush with grass and strawberries, a lover's delight. At the creeping gray dawn, Strawberry Hill smelled of ocean salt and earth and the air was heavy, ominous, as the chieftain's curse thrown to the same winds before he shivered and died.

If Mikhail had needed proof that the curse was still valid, he'd gotten it. After all, Ellie had arrived on his doorstep. At his parents' breakfast table, he had actually invited her to ruin what he had built—incomes depending on the success of the Amoteh Resort hung in the balance.

He stood at the crest of Strawberry Hill, jammed his hands in his peacoat and let the wind and rain tear at him as he looked over the black ocean and the lights of the small town below. In tourist season, the small town bustled and thrived, shopkeepers hurrying to restock their shelves. The scent of freshly baked sourdough bread mixed with salt air, chowders and hot dogs and Dungeness crabs at the Crab Shack. The charter boats would slide across the waves, the tourists' sails cutting into the blue sky.

A child's welfare hung in the balance; Hillary and Paul were no angels.

And Ellie's kiss had shot into him and twisted into a hungry, sensual knot simmering in him throughout the night. He didn't want to feel anything for Ellie but that fine regard one gives a potential disaster.

He could still taste her, feel her against him, feel that soft skin against his own, feel her breathe. Her hunger was real; she had opened to him, had given him all that a woman's lips could promise.

He'd been promised before and from a woman much like Ellie—too much like her. Once he'd thought that he'd paid the curse's price, the terrible fights with JoAnna, who craved city life and who did not hesitate to destroy the life within her.

Was he any better? Hadn't he wanted JoAnna for what she could do for his career, for the Amoteh? And he'd wanted her because his instincts had told him that it was time to create a home and a family.

But he'd loved her, or thought he did at the time, and his choice had been a disaster. He'd come away from his marriage wounded and fragile, and he never wanted to be torn apart again.

The chilly wind brought an admission Mikhail had circled for years: The failed marriage was his fault—he wasn't a perfect husband, devoting himself to a cause that JoAnna couldn't abide. He'd worked long hours and he'd known she was restless. He saw it in how she flirted with men. And sex—it never seemed complete, his body hungering for that link that never came, the bonding that went beyond the physical. As a friend and a lover and a husband, he'd left JoAnna unfulfilled. He couldn't share himself with her, his inner thoughts, nor did he honestly want to know hers.

JoAnna couldn't stand to have him touch her. She'd torment him sensually, but in the end, it was the same—frustrating, humiliating….

Ellie's kiss still burned him, tasting of her hunger.

Hunger. It rode him still, the feel of Ellie in his arms, the sounds and the scent of an aroused woman that set his instincts humming when he didn't think that possible. Even now, he wanted to find and claim her, and in truth, wanted her to claim him—maybe as a man, he needed that, the hunter needing the huntress.

Mikhail shrugged; he would have to watch his needs with Ellie. She could ignite his emotions like a flash fire, while he preferred to control them.

A gust of wind soared from the ocean, up the steep shelves of rock and grass that harbored birds' nests in the spring. The wind battered the dried sheaves of grass, rattling them, and then hit the man, who stood braced, legs wide apart.

Paul wasn't going to be happy if Ellie decided to stay. Meanwhile, she and Tanya were Mikhail's to protect.

So are you coming to work for me, or not? Mikhail had asked.

Three days later, Ellie stood in the shadows of the Stepanov living room, the big stone fireplace ablaze, gleaming on the wood paneling and hardwood floors, broken by thick woven rugs. The bold furniture and huge canvases of Mary Jo's Texas ranch and cattle scenes were softened by earth-, sea- and sky-colored pottery. Against one wall, the *samovar*, an elegant device to heat water for Russian *zavareka* or tea, was surrounded by beautiful matching cups and saucers. Fadey clearly loved this touch of the old country, looking like a man who had been blessed when served by his gracious wife.

In the evening after dinner, Mary Jo was happily rocking Tanya and telling stories of her Texas girlhood on the ranch. Fadey sat by the fire in his stocking feet, a contented man, his hands folded over his belly.

The Stepanov home was one of love and strength, proof that families could live together, love each other.

Ellie hadn't known exactly how exhausted she was, but the nights of deep sleep and the recovering naps throughout the days had proved just how long and hard she'd fought. Mikhail had not come to the house, and if his offer of a job held, she had no choice but to take it.

"Where do you think I'll find Mikhail?" she asked lightly. "We have business."

"Yes, of course," Fadey said. "At the shop. Take my coat, little one. There in the closet. Be careful on the path. It can be slippery. I will watch until you are there."

Outside, Ellie tugged Fadey's coat collar up around her throat, and inhaled the scent of wood, varnish, love and strength. She wasn't used to an open, caring family—*I will watch until you are there.*

Her mother had deserted her as a child. Ellie had grown up without any maternal influence, rarely touched by her father, just an ornament to complete his successful business picture. Fadey hugged, big strong arms enclosing her and lifting her off the ground as he kissed both cheeks. He laughed openly and teased Mary Jo slyly. He cuddled Tanya and put her upon his shoulders and told her that little girls were all princesses. Ellie had needed Fadey desperately, the affirmation that not all men were like her father, that some men loved their families deeply.

And in those three days, Tanya was blooming, growing, laughing. She needed a home and a family, not rented cabins and road miles in the back of a car. She needed the

warmth of Bliss and Ed, who doted on her with love beads
and kisses and hugs. She needed Ryan, Leigh's brother,
alias "Winter Child," to tickle and tease her. Most of all,
she needed what Ellie needed—to know that there were
strong, family men, like Jarek.

But dealing with Mikhail was another matter, Ellie
thought as she walked toward the Stepanov Furniture wood
shop. In the night, the lights were glowing in the massive
building.

Mikhail. As a woman, Ellie understood a man's need,
but Mikhail's had been too open, too raw and primitive,
torching her senses, challenging her and demanding. She'd
felt then as if the lid had been torn away to the man inside,
a passionate man. And a tender one as he held her later.
The contrast wasn't an easy one to fit inside the Mikhail
Stepanov she had known for years.

She braced herself at the big solid door of the furniture
shop. From inside came a blast of Russian music, and a
saw ripped at wood. With a deep breath, Ellie swung open
the door and stepped inside.

The passionate accordion music suited the man. Mikhail
was at the saw, a storm of sawdust flying around him,
caught by the lights overhead as he concentrated, frowning
at the wood in his big hands, guiding it on the course he
had set. Safety glasses shielded his eyes and he hadn't seen
her. He seemed wrapped in a savage fury, a private battle
within himself, not against the wood in his hands.

Ellie chose to step back into the shadows, beside a huge
armoire. That raw hunger sprung inside her instantly, heating....

Alone in his lair of wood furniture and surfboards, the
shelves of finishes and walls of tools, Mikhail moved almost gracefully, efficiently. In jeans and a T-shirt that
looked more like a rag than clothing, he wore a red bandanna wrapped around his forehead, a carpenter pencil
tucked above his ear.

Then, as if sensing he was being watched, he slowly

reached to switch off the saw, remove his safety glasses, and turned to stare at her. He reached for the tape player and the room was instantly silent. Too quiet, so quiet she could feel her humming, the prickle that being near Mikhail always brought, and her defenses rising.... "So you've chosen here to hide."

Old habits, she thought, the need to thrust at Mikhail, to make him react to her. She tried again, struggling to say what she really meant. "I don't want to keep you away from your family, Mikhail."

"I thought you needed time to think. And rest." He leaned back leisurely against the work counter and reached for a thermos, pouring liquid into a cup. "Coffee?"

"No, thanks." She stayed pressed back against the wall, sheltered by the huge block of furniture. Above them, the fluorescent lights hummed slightly as she summoned her courage and dropped her pride. "If you meant what you said about working for you, I'll take the job."

"I always mean what I say. You have the job."

"I don't want your pity. I will work, Mikhail. I'll really try." She didn't want to tell him about all the odd jobs she'd held, how much she'd had to learn about the simplest tasks she'd previously taken for granted.

"Yes, of course. I would not have an employee who did not."

Ellie jammed her hands in her pockets. She had to ask even more. "We need a place to stay."

He only nodded as she continued. "A place for Tanya and myself, if that's okay. I can't stay with your parents. One of the cheaper rooms will do just fine. You can take it out of my salary. I have to pay our way. I've...gotten very good at managing on little and I'll need working clothes. Tanya is outgrowing her clothes. I suppose there are thrift shops here?"

"Of course." He sipped the coffee and watched her, waiting. "You have the job, and we'll discuss your duties and compensation at my office in the morning. But you are staying at the Amoteh.''

"It's only temporary, Mikhail, then we'll move out. Leigh said that no one has rented Jarek's old cabin yet.''

He removed the red bandanna from his forehead and dropped it to the counter, as if dismissing her suggestion. "No washer or dryer…very primitive.''

"We've made do before. Tanya likes Laundromats.''

"Not this time,'' Mikhail said slowly and placed his cup on the counter. "Not for a while. I want you to be within reaching distance.''

He was so exact, so certain of himself, that Ellie could feel herself gearing up to argue. She walked to him slowly, arranging her thoughts. "It's because of that kiss, isn't it? You want…certain amenities from an employee?''

His gaze was lazy, his brief smile cold. "You know better.''

She did. While her father had done nothing about a young divorcée's plight, a mother with two small children fending off the threats of a Mignon top manager, Mikhail had. In the end, that mother replaced the manager and had performed better. What Paul tried to manage with threats and power, Mikhail accomplished with thoughtfulness and logic and, most of all, kindness. Dedication to Mikhail was far reaching in the Mignon chain; his connections with other managers were based on respect and friendship—they trusted him. Ellie did not doubt that if Paul and Mikhail warred on a corporate decision, Mikhail would win.

She trusted him, and, always independent, she feared that trust.

"You're still tired and on edge, Ellie. Let's do this tomorrow morning.''

She could have left, but instead she reached to brush the sawdust from his temple. Mikhail inhaled and tensed instantly, watching her, and the air between them was alive again, sizzling, waiting for the storm. Ellie placed her hand on his cheek, feeling the strong bones, the warm, rough flesh. She'd thought him unfeeling, a business machine, but now, she could almost feel his darkness: the failure of his marriage, the pain of losing his unborn child, whom he would have loved very deeply, passionately. Ellie wanted to soothe that ache, her fingers gliding back to his hair, smoothing it. "I'm sorry for what happened, Mikhail."

Mikhail's strong fingers circled her wrist and brought her hand to his lips. "I'll trade you. No pity for no pity."

She couldn't breathe, her heart racing. "Deal."

His lips burned, excited, dragging slowly, seductively, just parted across her palm. Mikhail leaned down to nuzzle her cheek with his. "You look like a little girl in that coat."

There was the surprising tenderness he'd shielded. "I'm not. Maybe I never was. I had to grow up fast.… I know quite a bit about you, you know. I read the detective's report in my father's files—he's like that, extending his tentacles into private lives. Your wife wasn't as private as you are."

"No, she wasn't. JoAnna was unhappy and didn't care who knew it. We fought."

His smile curved against her cheek and Ellie's body tensed, quivering just that once. "I know this is a bad situation for you. I'm sorry. But just a moment ago, you looked so fierce—I've never seen you like that. What are you fighting, Mikhail?"

"You," he said quietly, as he bent to gently kiss her. "I was fighting the taste, the feel and the scent of you. I think of you sleeping in my bed at the house and I want to be there with you."

So, Mikhail thought distantly, darkly, he was in pursuit of Ellie whether he liked it or not. Perhaps the chieftain's curse had tangled around him. It seemed his lot to choose another woman much like his ex-wife. A woman to twist him, to cut his pride, and yet he wanted her, his body hard now, aching for her softness and warmth.

Ellie stiffened and drew back, her face flushed, her eyes wary.

Terms, he thought, always a woman set terms for a man wanting her.

"She's in there, isn't she?" Ellie shot at him fiercely. "I see that look and I know you're thinking of your ex-wife. A socialite, wasn't she? Just like me? Wealthy? Just like I was? Maybe spoiled, too, just like me?"

Her hand grabbed the front of his shirt and a few painful hairs with the cloth and kissed him hard. "What we have between us, buddy, may not be nice, but it *is* honest. Fight me, kiss me, but make certain you're thinking about me. Don't go mucking up me with someone else."

Here was the fighter, the woman fierce in her anger and truth, and Mikhail admired her, wanted her even more. He couldn't help smiling. "Tomorrow, it's business. But be careful tonight."

The tilt to Ellie's chin said that she'd taken his warning as a challenge—but then, as only Ellie would, she served it back to him. "I can handle you, any time, Mikie."

"Please do, then. Handle me," Mikhail murmured, before he tugged her into his arms.

Ellie needed the chilly, damp night to steady her senses. Mikhail had offered to walk her to the Stepanov home, and the gesture was too old-fashioned, too courtly, for the man she had always pitted herself against.

Oh, there was plenty of that, she thought, remembering the deep, sensual kisses that still hummed in her body, the need to lay Mikhail out on that unfinished dining room table and—

She tugged up Fadey's coat. She was simply on edge, still dogged by exhaustion, and not up to Mikhail just now. He'd been too tender, cupping her head between his hands, slanting her head slowly, perfectly, to fit his lips. Those bone-melting kisses had slowly changed, and he'd unbuttoned her coat. Watching her, he'd smoothed her cheeks, her throat, and skimmed over her breasts.

Ellie could have purred, but just then she didn't know if she was breathing. She'd definitely floated as Mikhail's big hand had gently smoothed and cupped her breast.

His unsteady groan and the heat pouring from him could have warmed Ellie until the next century. The pounding of his heart coursed through her veins as she touched him, her hands skimming his chest beneath the shabby work shirt.

The tide lapped at the shoreline, the fog tingling on her face. Mikhail was a seductive beast, all right, once he got started, and always that raw passion simmered beneath....

She wanted to hold it in her hand, to claim him fiercely so that he would never look or think about another woman.

She laughed shakily to herself. *Handle me,* he'd invited. There certainly was a lot of him—aroused and close and...

A big man moved out of the shadows. "Mikhail?" she asked.

The voice was a sneer and coarse, and the mist carried the sharp tang of alcohol. "I'm the better man, honey. Lars Anders at your service. What's a pretty little thing like you doing out alone?"

"Walking." There was something frightening about that big, round face, those small eyes—the man was a predator, looking for weaker prey. She could feel him breathe, feel the coarse animal hunger inside him stir....

"Don't ignore me," he ordered and spun her around as she tried to walk past him.

Mikhail's too-quiet voice came from the night and suddenly he was beside her. "Leave her alone."

"Stepanov." The word was a dark curse slicing through the mist.

"Lars." Mikhail's voice was cold and firm. In that moment, Ellie sensed how dangerous he could be, how taut that powerful body had become, as if coiled....

"I was just walking—" Ellie began. Over her head, the two men were watching each other like fighters, ready to step into the ring. Lars was beefier, and she couldn't bear to see Mikhail get hurt.

Mikhail's arm went around her waist, placing her a little behind him. Clearly, Lars would have to deal with Mikhail to get to her. "Yes, of course. Good night, Lars."

But the man's small eyes darted from Mikhail to Ellie and back again. "So that's how it is. The great man has a woman. Your father took mine, and my brat."

"You abused them. He protected them."

Fury boiled in those small eyes, Lars's face puffing up. "All you Stepanovs—"

"Leave it." Mikhail turned Ellie firmly and wrapped his arm around her as they walked toward his parents' house. "Stay away from him, Ellie. He's bad news and he's got a grudge. If you need to walk at night, tell me."

Mikhail was silent and Ellie hurried to keep up with him. "You should have told him that we—that we aren't... I'm not your woman. It sounds so coarse."

"It would, from him."

Ellie's senses told her that Mikhail would cherish the woman he considered his and that was terrifying. He would want more than she had ever given....

At his parents' door, Mikhail smoothed back her hair and looked down at her, no longer grim and hard. "So then, the next time you need to walk and think, let me know, okay?"

He made her feel young and sweet and protected, a girl walked home by her sweetheart. Ellie found herself blushing and looking away.

"Hey. What's this?" he asked, smoothing her cheek.

She didn't understand his gentleness, his seeking look, that thumb cruising lightly over her hot cheek. Her emotions were all tumbling, churning, melting inside her. "I don't know."

"Sure you do." Mikhail bent to kiss her lightly, and

suddenly Ellie couldn't let him get away. She gripped his
coat and tugged him closer.

Mikhail's chuckle should have startled her, but it didn't.
She was too busy feasting on him.

Five

***

"**I** understand, exactly," Ellie said, as in his office, Mikhail reviewed her duties as his assistant. "Conference coordination and special activities. Focus on pushing Stepanov furniture, the local artisan work, and offering conference special, interesting activities, giving grand tours of the conference planning committees and, of course, making certain that conferences have shuttle facilities for tours—maybe afternoon sails. I've arranged all this before, for my father. Oh, yes, and big promotion for the celebrity charity golf tournament." She nodded as she ran through the notes on her pad of paper. "I understand that Edna is your secretary and that I am your assistant and that I am to inform her of my schedules so that our timelines can run smoothly. I will be working with you mostly in promotion and as a social director. I'll do a good job."

Dressed in his gray suit, Mikhail did not look like the man who had kissed her last night, or who had trembled in her arms, the sensual fever running between them. This morning, he was an employer introducing a new staff member to her duties. He unlocked the door to Bella Sportswear near the indoor swimming pool. Inside was a Mardi Gras of colored swimwear accessories.

"Leigh runs this, but you may have to step in. Leigh's contractions started this morning. She's two weeks early, but the doctor said she's okay."

"Oh, that's wonderful. She and the baby will be just fine."

"I think so, too. You'll have to do the best that you can with the shop. If it is false labor, then Leigh will be here to help show you around. Meanwhile, pick out something for you and Tanya from the shop."

"What we have is fine. Thank you." Ellie pushed away that twinge of shame that she hadn't provided better for Tanya, that secondhand clothing served the purpose.

"You'll need other things. Sunglasses, hats, totes, I want you to be a walking style show for anything available at the Amoteh. But nothing too…revealing. You walk, talk and think Amoteh."

"I see." He hadn't meant to insult her. When it came to the Amoteh, Mikhail was all business.

Just once, his gaze had taken in her long sleeve cream blouse and sweater, her loose, flowing navy slacks and walking loafers. She'd sold her suits, and on short notice, these clothes were her best for business. She'd learned how to make do and re-do with thrift-shop clothing, enough to get by until she could afford better.

Mikhail's nod said he approved of her clothing, good for moving around the Amoteh in the preseason. He touched her shoulder lightly, indicating the pool. "No swimming without lifeguards. Ryan, Leigh's brother, doubles up here sometimes. I do not wish to deal with wedding parties. Sobbing, frantic mothers of the brides are definitely your problem. My mother or Leigh usually handles them, but they're going to be busy. Where's Tanya?"

"At Bliss and Ed's, playing with their goat and learning

how to tie-dye T-shirts. I think there are plans for planting seeds in growing boxes. Leigh said that's exactly how she grew up—with lots of love and understanding, only in a van, not a small cottage. Tanya couldn't be happier."

"Not a bad way to grow up," Mikhail said quietly. "Do you like the suite?"

"It's perfect. Thank you." It was too close to his. "I'll be very careful not to bother you, Mikhail."

Mikhail looked out over the Pacific Ocean. "Too late. You already do. Make certain that Tanya is never alone, not even around a corner from where you can see her…that someone trustworthy is always with her. And if I'm not here, that you and she are moved into your suite tonight. I'm afraid my family can't be with you now."

Ellie frowned slightly and clicked her notebook closed. "This sounds more than a baby coming. Why are you so specific about Tanya? Of course I wouldn't let anyone untrustworthy near her."

Mikhail turned to look down at her. "I called Paul last night. He's not happy. I expect him to arrive any day. Or Hillary may come."

She'd trusted him and he'd betrayed her. Paul and Hillary would be on their way…. "You called him? *You called him?* How could you? You didn't even let—"

"They're not getting Tanya. She's going to be watched at all times. But with Leigh's baby on the way, we're going to keep this from her, from Bliss and Ed, and away from my parents. They know the situation and the danger, but now is the wrong time for Paul to start playing tough guy. I don't want them bothered by Paul's hot temper or Hillary's foul mouth. Your suite has top security devices and I've moved one of the single men into night duty. I want you moved in tonight."

"Or gone," she said, shaking with anger. Or was it fear?

"I didn't betray you, Ellie. I merely chose the battlefield. You can't keep running. I know about the attempts Hillary made to steal Tanya—once from the day care center while you worked. She's not above kidnaping. Paul will try other methods. Tanya stays here at night with us.''

Us...us... "You and me?"

Mikhail, the cool businessman, spoke quietly, firmly, logically. "Your suite opens into my apartment. Keep the door unlocked. If you need me, all you have to do is call. If I'm at the clinic, waiting for the baby, you have my beeper number. I expect you to use it if you have any trouble at all.''

Mikhail turned to view the ocean again. He'd placed his job and the Amoteh in danger...for a child.

Yet something else troubled him, and Ellie knew that it was the coming birth. She touched his arm and felt the muscles contract. "Leigh and the baby will be fine, Mikhail. Women are very strong when they have to be.''

"I know. Look what you have done. Are you going to let me help you?''

"Is the sky blue? Do I love chocolate and a bubble bath?'' she asked and wondered why she felt to dizzy and happy, just looking up at him.

Mikhail's expression changed, smoldered. "Keep looking at me like that and we're not going to make it through the day.''

"Threats and promises,'' she whispered.

He made a sound like a low, hungry, desperate growl. "Games? I wouldn't, if I were you.''

"You're not me. You're a step-by-step, righteous sort of guy. I'm impulsive.'' She grinned and reached up to pat his head, as if he were a little boy. Mikhail tensed and bristled so nicely beneath her touch, not at all like the methodical businessman he'd been moments before.

She turned and, with a smile, strolled away. She was woman. She was strong and fierce and wise and in control.

Mikhail stopped her with one word. It sailed across the empty pool to wrap around her like a lariat. "Lunch?''

Her warning senses started the flash. She'd teased Mikhail and now she wasn't certain. "In the kitchen? With Georgia? A learning tour? Sure."

"In my apartment? Now?" His voice was a husky, sensual invitation she wasn't ready to take.

"Sorry. I'm going driving on the golf course. Sand trap inspection, you know." She continued walking, but the sound of his chuckle followed her.

Two tense weeks later, mid-March sunshine slid though the windows of Jarek's new home. Leigh sighed luxuriously and lay back on the recliner covered with a sheet. "I've gone to heaven. No hovering husband, just girl talk. A pedicure, manicure, a facial and my favorite soap opera on television. I can cry all I want when Jonas is unfaithful with his sister-in-law and his daughter is blackmailing the chauffeur, with whom she had an affair, and his mother has forged his name on contracts he doesn't want for kickback money.... And Katerina is being pampered by Mary Jo and Bliss. I think she's going to have Mary Jo's green eyes, just like Mikhail and Jarek.... Thanks, Ellie. I love my family dearly, and my baby, but I really needed this."

Ellie placed her hand against the window of Leigh and Jarek's home, overlooking the beach. The afternoon was warm and on the beach, Tanya ran to discover whatever the tide had left. Grinning, she scampered back to show her shells to Fadey, who was obviously enjoying himself as he picked up the little girl and whirled her around. He tossed her lightly into Jarek's arms, then Jarek nuzzled her playfully before passing her to Mikhail.

That was how Mikhail had handled Ellie, after their first kiss, tossing her lightly to Fadey. *I kissed her. She liked it, and now she's mad.... She wants me, of course.*

Of course she wanted Mikhail. She wanted to run him down, stake him out and devour him until he was helpless.

Ellie rubbed her arm. But Mikhail had never been helpless, and she could be the one to be devoured, an experience she wasn't likely to forget.

Leigh came to stand beside Ellie, watching the big men play with the little girl. "I grew up like that, racing and playing and loved. Most of all, I was loved. Bliss and Ed liked to follow the winds of the universe, and for a time, as an adult, I resented it. But now I know that I had the best of everything—love. Um…I should warn you that Bliss and Ed think children shouldn't be burdened by clothing in warm weather. Most of the time, I just wore love beads and sunshine."

In the sunshine, Mikhail had knelt to examine Tanya's collection, and the little girl stood beside him, her arm looped loosely around his neck.

The peaceful scene contrasted sharply with Hillary's burning, erratic calls to Ellie. "I'm going to get my kid, one way or the other."

Paul's call had been fierce and brisk, and he didn't waste threats or empty words. He would make good his promise to rip the Amoteh from Mikhail and shatter the incomes of people depending on him. And he would take his time, making Ellie wait. Paul knew how to build fear of reprisals.

"Let's just play this game out, shall we?" Mikhail had said easily as he worked on business in her suite. Asleep in the other room, Tanya was always well watched. Like most rooms in the Amoteh, Ellie's suite was furnished with Stepanov furniture, bold against the softer shades of mauve and cream. Just like the family, it was made to last, and the linens and bathroom soaps and oils all bore the strawberry logo. The small fireplace was perfect, guarding against the cold mist outside; the kitchen tiny and complete and the business work center well fixed with a computer and faxing and intercom facilities.

During the evenings, as they worked, listing ideas for the promotions and conferences, the door to Mikhail's apartment was open, and he was very proper about knocking before entering. He'd sit beside her on the sprawling cream couch, comfortable in jeans and stocking feet and concentrating on meshing their ideas. Mikhail took every idea and turned it around carefully, asking questions before either approving or rejecting.

Mikhail hadn't touched Ellie, and she missed him. He had returned to the cool methodical businessman, and she was too busy getting the feel of the Amoteh, and exploring the possibilities for conferences and entertainment. They worked together well—if she followed his orders, which she was doing for now. She had other ideas she hadn't told him, ones that she knew he would squash.

It was only a temporary situation, Ellie decided. She knew what Mikhail thought of her, that she'd been rich and spoiled, a society jet-setter just like his ex-wife, not likely to stay...but then, her past performances with him hadn't been exactly sweet. And it was so hard to be good around Mikhail. When he looked so withdrawn, concentrating on business, she just wanted to grab his tie, wrap it around her fist and tug him to her for a kiss.

She wanted to burn herself into his mind and body so that he wouldn't forget her. Maybe that was what she wanted all along...to have Mikhail's full attention, to meet him there in the passion that simmered now in her.

Leigh held Ellie's hand as they watched the men and the child on the beach. Leigh sighed luxuriously and said, "The Stepanovs are a wonderful family and Mikhail is a lovely man. He needs you—you make him feel alive. Anyone can see what's happening between you."

"He doesn't trust me—as a woman. I can feel it. Maybe I deserve that, given the Ellie I used to be—self-serving, spoiled and all the rest. I'm asking a lot of him."

"Not any more than Jarek or Fadey would give. Stepanov men were meant to protect and to love, but Mikhail had little of that in his marriage. JoAnna put him through hell. It tore his heart out to know she destroyed his baby. She wasn't faithful, and I have to question if it even *was* his baby. Yet he grieved for it as if it were. And he took the divorce as a failure. Failure is so hard for Mikhail to accept."

Leigh was very quiet, and then she said fiercely, "I would do anything to protect my husband from those feelings, the dark, brooding side of their Stepanov heritage. Jarek's first wife died, and he felt so guilty, felt that he should have gone with her to Strawberry Hill to conceive a child that day. I danced in front of the chieftain's grave, because if there is a curse, I didn't want it to touch Jarek again. Maybe it was silly, but I love him so. I knew myself—what was really important—my love for Jarek, and that's what they say will break the curse, a woman who knows her own heart."

"Really? You did that?"

"I had to tear him away from her, from his guilt. I know it was silly to believe in a curse, but it always seems to hover here, people talk of it. I would have done anything to tear her from him."

Ellie shook her head. "It wasn't silly at all. I'd use anything I could to keep Tanya safe."

Leigh yawned delicately. "I could use a nap, and from the looks of you, Ellie, you could, too. Mikhail said you need hard work because you're afraid for Tanya, but Mary Jo says you're working too hard. And then you're so sweet to take time to pamper me."

Ellie thought of how Hillary had reacted after childbirth, as though she deserved every homage. "I'd better go and let you get some rest."

"Ellie, thank you so much for all you've done. The baby quilt you made for Katerina is just beautiful."

"I like to sew. There hasn't been much time for that, but it settles me. I borrowed Georgia's machine."

On the way back to the Amoteh, Ellie scanned Strawberry Hill. It would be hours before she would take Tanya back to the suite that was now their home. Tanya was to go back to the Stepanov home to enjoy baby Katerina. And Ellie needed all the good luck she could get....

Mikhail pushed up the rocky trail on Strawberry Hill. In late afternoon, the wind had kicked up, dark clouds forming on the horizon, as if Chief Kamakani was gathering his powers—and Ellie was missing. Norm, the head grounds-keeper, had said that she had asked the way to Strawberry Hill and Kamakani's gravesite.

With a storm brewing, the clouds skimming shadows over the water, Ellie could be pushed off the cliff by a gust of upward wind, knocked flat and hit her head on a stone.... Mikhail pushed away his fears, and hurried upward, stumbling once and cutting his hand on a sharp rock.

The wind caught the swaying tops of the pines and hissed through them. Breathing hard, Mikhail reached the summit. The wind flattened Ellie's jacket to her, sending her hair out in a storm of gleaming silk. She stood braced against the force, her head lifted, as though she welcomed the wind, embraced it.

A cold shaft of fear shot through Mikhail. More than one woman had obsessed about the chieftain, including Jarek's first wife.

Ellie turned to him and his heart leaped, beating furiously. "What are you doing here?"

"Thinking. Why don't you want me?"

Why don't you want me? The question pounded at him, and a gust of wind sailed against them, carrying her scent to him—erotic, fresh, feminine....

"Want you?" he asked grimly, before tugging her to him and holding her safe within his arms. A seagull swept too close, driven by the wind, as though the chieftain were threatening—

She pushed at him, her hair flying around her face. "I'm not her, Mikhail. I'm me."

"And I'm not your father—he rejected you, didn't he? Don't apply that to me."

A toss of her head threw her hair into the wind, pulled back from her face, those dark thunderstorm eyes flashing at him. "Prove it."

She always right there, edgy and pushing and fascinating

and wild and woman, stirring his senses, making him react in the most primitive ways. "I wanted to give you time to rest, to adjust. Most of the time, you look like you haven't slept. And I don't want your gratitude or payback. Let's keep this clean, shall we? Apart from the situation with Tanya's safety."

"Always so logical," she murmured, and pushed away again, freeing herself. She began to run across the fields that would be lush with strawberries, and Mikhail found himself in pursuit, his senses pounding to catch her, to hold her, to feel her close and warm and alive against him.

She turned to glance at him over her shoulder, and it wasn't fear he read in her expression. It was excitement and flirtation, a woman beckoning to a man. Who was the hunter and who was the prey? he wondered just that once before catching her and lifting her high in his arms.

Ellie laughed then, her hair flying around her face, her cheeks pink and her eyes soft and glowing upon him. She was his enchantress, and inside him, the tempo rose—he was a man needing to claim the woman haunting him.

He could feel the music inside him, wild and passionate, and hungry, so hungry, storming in his blood, the heat rushing around them, man and woman.

Her arms around his neck, she watched him as he carried her to a flat rock, still bearing the warmth of the sun, laying her gently down, to cover her with his body. "Why did you run from me?" he asked.

"Maybe I was running from myself," Ellie replied. "From this. There are parts of myself I've always kept to myself, and you're too thorough. You see too much."

"I want to see more."

Ellie reveled in Mikhail's weight, in the way his thumbs stroked her temples as they stared at each other. She could feel the passion in him, the heat and the desire, the powerful emotions and body held in check as he watched her. But there was tenderness there, too, lurking in his smile. "Happy?" he asked.

She squirmed a little beneath him, enjoying the sturdy feel of his body, the strength and warmth of it over her own, though she knew he braced his full weight away. Mikhail was a protective, thoughtful man. "You're so easy."

His eyebrow hitched up, mocking her. "Easy, am I?"

She stroked that eyebrow with her fingertip. "Terribly easy. I could have you, if I wanted you."

His kiss was slow, deep and thorough, leaving her body pounding hungrily. "Could you?" he asked in a husky drawl.

Ellie smoothed his hair, toying with it, and traced the sharp slash of his cheekbones. He toyed with her earlobe, smoothing it. "No earrings? I remember diamonds."

"Sold them. They were part of the picture Paul wanted. It didn't hurt a bit." Her breath hitched as Mikhail's teeth prowled her lobe, his unsteady breath sweeping across her skin as his hands moved lower, stroking her waist, the denim covering her hips.

He turned, lying beneath her, and she dived into him, feasted on his skin, his scent, his mouth, her hands fisting his hair. She wanted to mark Mikhail as hers, to tear away the pain of another woman.

"Little savage," he whispered rawly as she nipped his bottom lip and then licked it.

"Look who's talking." She couldn't help moving against him, the pressure building between them until the air sparked and churned and heated. Mikhail's face was shadowed, dark and closed, holding away from her what she would have, his eyes slitted, looking up at her.

She was half in love with him now, she realized, as somewhere off in the distance the wind howled and cold rain began to slash at them. Had they always been moving toward this time, this reckoning, as she'd slashed at him and he'd grimly refused to enter her game?

It wasn't a game now. It was raw and quivering, tender and hungry, because they'd tasted each other and knew....

Mikhail was on his feet, tugging her up to him. His impatience was new and she reveled in his desire for her. They hurried down the path, his arm around her. He opened her car door and bent to kiss her. "Turn on the heater. You're soaked."

Mikhail's black BMW followed her car as she drove to the Amoteh, still quaking with the need to hold him, to keep him safe and to protect him. She frowned into the rearview mirror, the curtain of rain between his car and hers. More ran between them than desire, and she wasn't certain of the tenderness that Mikhail could make her feel. Her father had taught her not to trust that emotion.

The Amoteh was quiet and sprawling, as Mikhail quickly built a fire in her suite and she took off her damp coat. "I'll get something to eat," he said quietly and turned to her. "You're cold—"

He stopped and rose slowly, staring at her body, at her breasts where her nipples thrust against the light turquoise sweater. Her heart seemed to slow and wait as he walked toward her, then curved his hand around the back of her neck, drawing her close to him.

In his eyes, she saw an age-old question, that of a man asking for a woman, desiring her. "Yes," she whispered into the silence, the heat simmering between them.

Mikhail would be very thorough, she thought desperately, too hungry for him, as he slowly eased her sweater from her and considered her breasts beneath the lace. He breathed roughly, just that sharp intake of breath, as he unsnapped and unzipped her jeans. She slipped out of her loafers and he stroked away her jeans until she stood only in scraps of lace.

She half feared Mikhail's dark, intent look, and yet, as a woman, she reveled in it.

Ellie didn't expect the tug on her bra strap, the pressure enough to snap it and the other as Mikhail's big hands passed lightly over her, caressing away her briefs. Her hands beneath his blood-red sweater roamed that rough hot flesh, needing him pressed against her, all that wonderful big body trembling for her as she was for him.

Mikhail tore off his sweater, tossing it aside, and stripped away his jeans. Firelight defined his body, all hard planes and cords and muscles and jutting power. She could almost feel him throb with desire, her own body softening, waiting.

It would be no easy, forgettable lovemaking, she knew, as his fingertips began to prowl as if taking her into him, sensually absorbing her, his hands cradling her breasts, smoothing her stomach and hips and brushing her just there... She gripped his arms, fingers digging in as her legs weakened, the pounding within her a storm of emotions.

While he could appreciate and be thorough, her hunger ran too fiercely; she was a woman used to taking what she wanted. She'd waited a lifetime for this man, and now...

"You are already—" Mikhail's voice was deep, raw, raising her senses, her need of him.

He eased her to the carpet in front of the fire and settled over her as he had on the rock. This time, the storm was inside her, the cold rain replaced by the heated pounding of her blood, the hunger.

His hands were gentle, seeking, claiming, his lips moving over her with a certainty that she knew could never be erased. The hot suction of his mouth, the lave of his tongue, sent her arching against him, a fierce, driving need too poignant to wait.

Mikhail seemed to gently flow over her, the muscles of his powerful back taut beneath her hands. She met his stare above her as he moved intimately, carefully, giving her time to adjust.

"Mikhail..." she whispered when they were complete, one locked with the other.

His words were dark and stormy and fierce, the bunching of his shoulders, his taut body pressing against hers, said he was forcing himself to wait for her.

But Ellie's body raced on furiously, helplessly, clenching Mikhail. When she opened her eyes, she found Mikhail's tender look, his thumb brushing away the tears from her lids. "You went inside yourself, taking everything."

She tried to smile, mocking her emotions as she had for a lifetime. "I'm greedy."

He smoothed her cheek. "Even now, as you hold me deep and tight, you are shy of me. Why?"

She looked away at the fire and Mikhail's hand gently brought her back to him. "It's new. It's different. There's just more…" she answered simply. "I'm terrified."

"So am I. We can stop."

"You would do that? Now?" *Who was he? Who was this man, so intense, so concerned for her above his own needs?*

"Of course."

She moved slightly, feeling the heaviness of him within her, and Mikhail tensed. "I've got you now," she whispered, pressing her fingers against his back, enjoying the flow of the power there—the controlled power, waiting for her.… "You're not going anywhere."

"Oh, no?" There was that challenge, that arrogance she adored.

"Mikhail. If you leave me now, I'll—"

His searing kiss sent her body flying toward his, her arms holding him tight. And then the storm began, the heat flashing, her blood pounding. She took what he gave and served it back to him as they climbed higher. Mikhail… Mikhail…Mikhail…

Later, she would hold him and wonder at the peace she had found, the safety and the comfort within his arms.

She'd been alone all of her life, and to think that Mikhail was a part of her now was frightening—because there was no going back, ignoring the beauty of what had just happened.

She stroked his hair and kissed his forehead, settling beneath the afghan he had drawn over them.

"You're thinking too hard," he said sleepily as he drew her closer and his hands began to roam. "Think about this...."

Later, at the Stepanov home, the family shared *zavarka* in front of the fire while Leigh contentedly nursed Katerina. Mikhail couldn't help watching Ellie, the blush that would course up her cheeks as their eyes met, and their bodies remembered and hummed.

On impulse, he rose from his chair and plucked Ellie from hers, carrying her back to sit on his lap. "Mikhail, don't..." she whispered frantically, trying to push free of him.

He felt like a boy, excited and a little in love with his first sweetheart, and he wrapped his arms around her and nuzzled her neck until she wriggled and laughed. When she was breathless and limp and leaning back in his arms, the softness flew around them again, the other thing that they both feared.

Ellie reached to smooth his hair and then his cheek, and the haunting loneliness in him gentled. Mikhail took her hand to bring it to his lips, and the magic deepened and caressed.

They'd made love desperately, gently, and yet—yet more awaited, then he thought, as he looked up to see his family watching them, smiling.

With a delighted squeal, Tanya climbed up to sit on his other knee. "Do that to me, Mikhail. Mom never laughs like that. She sounds like a girl."

"She is a girl, a very pretty one, just like you." Mikhail nuzzled the little girl's neck until she laughed and twisted away, running to leap on Ryan, who took her to the floor, tickling her.

"It's good," Fadey said quietly as he studied his son. Fadey's look said he knew that Mikhail had found the woman he wanted and had claimed her.

"Very good," Mikhail agreed as he held Ellie closer.

She studied him slowly, and he could have fallen into those dove-gray eyes. ''I'm not used to this…this openness. You say what you feel,'' she whispered.

Not always, Mikhail thought, remembering the shadows he preferred not to share with his family, the bitter fights with his ex-wife, the grief over his unborn child. But they knew and understood.

''Sometimes the quiet is good, too,'' he said, drawing her head down on his shoulder and letting peace roll over him as smoothly as a gentle, sunlit tide.

He nuzzled Ellie's silky hair and welcomed the warmth and the scent, the softness, the rightness of her in his arms.

But he knew that even now, after making love, she was fighting any future with him, throwing up barricades. She'd learned in a lifetime how to protect herself from the pain that came from caring for men whose capacity for love wasn't equal to her own.

Mikhail understood her reasoning, but he wouldn't hurt her—ever. He intended to give her all the love that was within him.

The Silhouette Reader Service™ — Here's how it works:

NO POSTAGE
NECESSARY
IF MAILED
IN THE
UNITED STATES

BUSINESS REPLY MAIL
FIRST-CLASS MAIL   PERMIT NO. 717-003   BUFFALO, NY

POSTAGE WILL BE PAID BY ADDRESSEE

SILHOUETTE READER SERVICE
3010 WALDEN AVE
PO BOX 1867
BUFFALO NY 14240-9952

Six

The next morning in his office, Mikhail replaced the telephone and grimly considered Paul's bitter threats—"I'll jerk that resort off that godforsaken stretch of beach so fast, you won't know what hit you. By the time my bulldozers get done, nothing will be left but bald, scraped dirt and a dried-up town no one wants to visit. If you don't play ball, your career with Mignon is finished. I'll ruin you."

"Not if I can help it," Mikhail said quietly as he sipped the Amoteh's house blend coffee.

Paul would take his time—because he liked to play on and build fear—but he was capable of carrying out his threats. Mikhail had already set his defense in motion, contacting other Mignon resort managers. He had helped most of them deflect Paul's bullying at one time or another. If there was one thing Paul appreciated, it was good managers who were "worth their weight in gold."

It was a sad thing, Mikhail thought, that Paul didn't appreciate his family as much as he did a finely tuned organization.

Mikhail hadn't seen Ellie this morning, and it was usual for her to deliver Tanya to Mary Jo or Leigh or Bliss before starting work. He had thought about holding her all night, hoarded each memory of sounds and fever and touch, how she had touched him, trembling at first and then with a certainty and strength he hadn't suspected....

Mikhail had ached to go to her this morning, but he held back because just the sight of her all tousled and warm could have made him ache more....

And they were about to enter a battle where he had to think clearly.

He smiled briefly at Edna, who was straightening the papers that needed his morning attention. A widow providing for her ailing sister, Edna's character matched the prim suit and blouse she wore—ever meticulous and efficient. "The guard dog," salesmen had often called his secretary. She was good at her job, discreet, honorable, sensible—and tough, Mikhail added, a woman to respect.

"A mixed bouquet was a perfect choice, Mikhail," Edna said firmly. "They've been delivered to her suite. When she returns to it, Ellie is in for a nice surprise."

Mikhail pictured Ellie in a sturdy Stepanov bed, flushed, curved and drowsy amid the rose petals they had just crushed. The tight squeeze of her body had warned him against more yesterday. He wanted to be very careful with her, not only sensually, but in the way a woman should be treated—cherished. Perhaps a little old-fashioned, but as a Stepanov, it was his right to cherish a woman with whom he had made love and still wanted.

Mikhail slashed his name across the papers, approving a percentage raise for the employees. "She is a surprising woman. You realize the situation, Edna? Ellie's sister and her father are not going to be sweet. They want Tanya for a business pawn."

"Over your dead body," Edna said lightly. "And mine.

That little girl is a ray of sunshine, too sweet for Paul Lathrop. I cannot understand how he could possibly spawn two daughters so opposite. I've met them both, and Ellie is that child's rightful mother, not Hillary. You're right to protect them.''

''There are jobs at stake here, Edna. Including yours.'' Mikhail began inspecting the additional papers she had prepared for his signature.

''I'm not worried. You'll handle it, Mikhail. I know what it cost Ellie to ask you for help. You won't let her down, and she knows it. She's strong herself, but now and then, everyone needs a little help—like you helping me get this job when I needed support for myself and my sister.''

''You're a top right hand, Edna. You helped yourself.''

''So will Ellie. Life's a struggle, and when she's on her feet, Ellie will thank you.''

Mikhail frowned slightly and looked at Edna, who had known him since he was a little boy. ''I don't want her to feel obligated.''

''She knows how to separate the wheat from the chaff, Mikhail. Give her credit.''

Automatically, as he worked on the papers, Mikhail outlined the day to Edna. Then, suddenly, a click of the office's heavy doors took his attention to Ellie's curved backside.

As she backed into his office with a loaded cart, her slacks were tight against her bottom—a round, soft curve that he had cupped in both hands as they made love. Every molecule in his body tuned into a sensual knot.

Then he realized that Edna was speaking to him and that he had just broken the pen in his hand—the ink was dripping on the paper.

''I'll deal with this,'' Edna said crisply, sweeping up the papers and taking a moist towelette from his drawer. She wiped the ink drops from his hand as if he were a little boy, smiled with what he suspected was delight and patted him on the head.

Then Edna moved to hold the door open for Ellie, who was still tugging the cart inside. When the door closed, Ellie straightened and whipped off the cloth over the elegant *samovar*. Splashed with gold and flowers, the Russian device to make tea was complete with a teapot on top and an ornate spigot.

She sat on the chair in front of his desk, her expression grim.

"What's this?" he asked.

"I ordered this *samovar*. I thought we would have an elegant tea, complete with Russian tea cookies. High tea is very popular with ladies. Some men might like it, too. Fadey does, and so does Jarek. I think it is very appropriate, and Edna approved the purchase. And it's beautiful, quite the softening complement for your office. There's nothing that settles a good snarl like a civilized cup of tea. We'll need china, of course, or those decorative metal holders for glasses. We could offer a proper tea to the menu for guest rooms, complete with a strawberry tea cozy—all of which we could sell in the resort's shop."

Mikhail cut through Ellie's new product ideas to what mattered most—her opinion of him. "I see. You think I snarl."

"You brood. I've upset your kingdom. You don't like changes. Call it a silent snarl." Her brisk tone said she had come to a decision and a bottom line. Last night's kiss at her door had told him she was already in flight, moving back from what had happened, from him as a man, as a lover. The circles under her eyes said she hadn't slept and Mikhail ached to hold her.

"You're this—" Ellie pointed to the *samovar*. "The Stepanovs are based on old-fashioned love and respect and traditions that they pass on to their children—like hugs and kisses and understanding. My family isn't."

"So, you've been thinking, is that it?" Mikhail's nerves danced and chilled. Ellie had the look of a woman in retreat—from him. Her tone said she was laying out realities that couldn't be dismissed…or overcome.

"Exactly. I take responsibility for my actions. I wanted you. I took you. Let's just leave it at that. This is a temporary situation, and you've provided us with a safe haven for now. For that, I'm grateful."

Mikhail rose slowly and fought the stormy mood inside him. He now knew the battle—her fear that they weren't a match, that their backgrounds separated their futures. But yesterday afternoon there hadn't been any boundaries. "It isn't gratitude that I want from you."

She wasn't as unaffected as she seemed. Ellie's hands gripped the arms of her chair, her knuckles showing through the fair skin. She sat ramrod straight, her body tense. The light passing through the window set fire to her hair, and Mikhail wanted to…to kiss her until she forgot about any differences between them, and any danger. "Do you trust me, Ellie? Yes or no."

Her gray eyes warily flicked to him and away. "Yes *and* no," she responded carefully. "I always thought you were one thing, and now I find another."

He came to stand by her chair, fighting the impulse to drag her to him. "Do you trust me as a man?"

She sat rigid in the chair, staring away from him. "I have a hard time with trust, Mikhail. I'm sure you can understand why."

A bitter pain sliced through him. They had loved and touched and met on a plane that meant he would want her forever, long past the heated desire of their bodies. "So that's it, darling. You wanted me. You took me. No regrets. End of story."

She breathed deeply and her breasts lifted and filled her sweater. "You're an emotional man, Mikhail. You come from passionate people. Mine have ice water for blood. You know Paul, and then there's my mother—dear Nora. He basically bought her and discarded her for a younger model. She didn't care. The settlement was enough to make her leave me with him, because Paul never loses assets. That's what Hillary and I were, business assets.''

He ached for the damage Paul had done, and reveled in how Ellie had survived and achieved, in her capacity for love despite how little had been given her.

Mikhail circled her, wrapped in his frustration. "You complicate a simple matter. We made love, and you're frightened. It's only natural. I should have been more thoughtful. In my hunger, I forgot a woman needs time to adjust. We've been busy, and I should have taken time for you. I apologize."

Her soft hands flexed on the chair, though she didn't look at him. "No apologies needed. I was thinking, weighing, and it was right for me—with you. You're helping protect Tanya, for now, and I need to be honest with you about my feelings. I really tried with my marriage, Mikhail. Logically, it should have worked, even without him wanting Tanya. We were well suited. We played our parts perfectly, but I'm not good at lasting relationships. That's why I used to keep them on the light side. It was so much easier. Looking back, I probably left those relationships before they really began. My ex-husband accused me of being a tease and frigid. There's probably truth in that. I thought it would be easy, that we knew our roles and what to expect from each other.''

Ellie definitely wasn't frigid, rising to a fever pitch in their lovemaking, searing him with her hunger and melting after the fullest completion of lovemaking. Now her mind was at work, cutting away at the beauty, fearing it. "You think I will want too much, more than you want to give," he told her.

She folded her hands on her lap, studying them as she spoke quietly. "I found that sex, giving my body, actually meant more than a marriage duty. I wasn't...linked.''

Mikhail settled back into his thoughts. He knew exactly what she meant; he had experienced the same feeling. They had been "linked," and not only in body; for that time they had been one being, with one heart—finally complete.

Yesterday Ellie had not teased, and she was definitely not cold. She was fighting for Tanya, and yet it hurt her to battle with her family, because her love ran deep.

"Be aware that you mean little to me—personally," he lied, changing tactics and prodding at her. He had ached for her throughout the night, and perhaps his entire life had been a search for this one woman. "I'm set for a takeover, Ellie. You and Tanya are just pawns in what I want. So don't get any mistaken ideas that my family breeds honor, any more than yours."

She was on her feet in a heartbeat, taut and furious with him, anger alight in her hair, her skin, snapping in her eyes. "Don't you dare say that about Fadey and Mary Jo. Nor Jarek or Leigh. Just don't you dare."

"We're a match, you and I, are we not? Cold? Bloodless? Heartless?" he asked, pushing her, excitement flowing through him that only Ellie could ignite.

She threw up her hands. "How can you say that? You developed this resort out of nothing. It's beautiful and magnificent and— You built the Amoteh because you wanted employment for those you love, and security and health benefits, and—"

Ellie caught his tie and wrapped it around her fist as Mikhail let her back him against the wall.

The fire was there, the real woman, and Mikhail adored her, this woman, his woman. They stared at each other, the air heating between them, shifting with remembered shadows of their lovemaking, the intimacy. "You're the only man who can set me off like this, Mikhail," Ellie said unsteadily, after a moment.

"Likewise." He couldn't help grinning and bent to kiss her knuckles. The slender hand flattened against his chest moved in a light caress, pleasing him yet more. "So I am the only one, hmm?"

Ellie scowled up at him, her eyes stormy and her color

almost as high as when they had made love. "Arrogant, spicy, delicious, moody—"

He kissed her hand again and reveled in her frustration and anger, a reflection of his a moment ago. "Go back to the spicy part. Like pepper, or cinnamon, or...?"

Ellie threw away his tie and looked disgusted as she folded her arms over her chest. "Exotic. Flavorful, full-bodied flavor, that sort of thing. I couldn't sleep last night, and you're the reason. By the way, we need a tennis and a golf pro to give lessons here at Amoteh."

"Too expensive. Now back to the point—it's interesting to be compared to a coffee. Tell me more about how flavorful I am. Am I full-bodied and fulfilling to the taste?"

Ellie stared at him. "I will not."

"You will, darling." Mikhail moved to lock his office door and to punch Edna's number on the intercom. "Hold my calls."

He thought he heard his prim secretary giggle before he turned his attention to Ellie. He ripped off his tie and tossed it aside; the tie was followed by his jacket and shirt. On his way back to Ellie, he kicked off his shoes. "I want to make certain that we never have this conversation again, where you come in here looking like a thundercloud and run through all that garbage and setting up fences between us. I want you as a woman, not as a pawn. The question is, how do you want me? As a momentary distraction and then you go on your merry way?"

"I've hurt you. That wasn't my intention." Her voice trembled as Mikhail jerked the drapes closed, shadowing the room.

"Yes. But, of course, you hurt me. How did you think I would take your little declaration about how unsuitable we are on the morning after we made love? If it's a cold, needy thing between us, darling, prove it. If what you are trying to tell me is so, sex could be as routine as opening morning mail...dispense with the necessities and get on with the day."

"Mikhail, I didn't mean it like that. You're so... upsetting."

"So I upset you, do I? Good," he said darkly, and noted with satisfaction that she wasn't afraid of him as he came to stand close to her.

"You big, dumb, goofy—" Ellie said as she reached for him.

Mikhail caught her to him, lifting her off her feet, holding her so that their eyes were level. "You are not your mother or your sister, who would desert or sell a child for their own welfare. You are not like Paul."

Ellie fought tears; she'd battled a lifetime of fear that she would be exactly like her family. She'd fought Paul's cold ridicule, his derision that she wasn't the son he wanted. She'd grown brittle, tough and wary of genuine emotion; she naturally reacted sword for sword. "I could be. I like having my way."

He was giving her too much: warmth, tenderness, forgiveness. And she had hurt him, just as he'd been hurt before.

Mikhail kissed her lightly, his expression tender. "And I like having mine."

He eased into a big chair, holding her on his lap. His large, gentle hands stroked her body, caressing her thighs and breasts. "I missed you last night. How do you feel this morning? I mean, I did not want to hurt you. You are so small—"

His touch trembled now, seeking beneath her sweater, just as her body softened and ached and warmed....

Mikhail was very warm, and aroused, frowning slightly as he concentrated on cupping her breast, running his thumb across the tip. She wanted to dive into him, to soothe and comfort and take at the same time. Ellie didn't know how to express her emotions; she just knew they fluttered and tingled inside her, deeper than she had ever felt, terrifying and yet fascinating her. "You haven't hurt me, Mikhail. Um, could you please do whatever you're thinking about?''

"I want to give you time," he whispered rawly as he leaned her back to kiss her throat. "But I also want to give you something else."

His mouth cruised open and hot against her skin as he eased away her sweater and bra. The hunger in his kiss became her own, and when his mouth suckled gently, his hand moving inside her slacks, caressing her, Ellie felt the warming of her blood, the storm swirling in her body, the rhythm sweeping her away into the fire as she gripped Mikhail's shoulders, her nails digging in to anchor the surging tide flowing over her.

His lips muffled her startled, keening cry, and his hands gentled her down to earth again. She rested against him, spent by her passion. He was still hard beneath her, his eyes glittering, his features taut with desire and tenderness. She doubted that she could move from him; her bones seemed to be melting inside her. Mikhail was very thorough. "That wasn't exactly fair, Mikhail. I'll have to pay you back. But right now, you've done your deed."

"So have you, apparently. It is quite a sight to watch, you blooming with my touch. I can only await the pleasure, though I cannot guarantee all those fascinating little sounds," he murmured dryly.

Ellie prepared to leave his office, then leaned against the door and looked at him. Mikhail understood the sensual, warm hunger that ran through her now—because it ran through him, also. "Hold that thought," he said softly, "or stay and make it come true."

With a smile that said she intended to do her best when they wouldn't be disturbed, Ellie left his office. Moments later, Edna entered Mikhail's office.

"Lovely day, isn't it, Edna?"

Edna turned to the window and noted the dreary, chilling rain. "Oh, absolutely lovely."

Mikhail's smiled as he slashed through paperwork, a man

eager to be done. His tie was tucked into his jacket pocket, and his dress shirt was tossed over a chair. Life was good, he decided, thinking of the satiny bra beneath his shirt, and the way Ellie had quivered upon his lap, flushed and warm and pleasuring him.

"Lovely day, Mikhail," Edna repeated lightly as the storm outside began to claw at the window's glass.

He interrupted his humming, scanned the day outside and smiled. "Perfect."

That afternoon, Mikhail stood rigidly aside as the future bride's crying mother left Ellie's office. Ellie glimpsed Mikhail's momentary horrified expression as Mrs. Hightower grabbed him and backed him against the wall. She sobbed against his chest. "You're Mikhail Stepanov, aren't you?"

"Yes. I'm certain everything will be fine," he said stiffly, obviously uncomfortable.

"My little girl. I'm losing my little girl," the woman sobbed as Ellie came to stand at the door, her expression amused.

Mikhail shot her a narrow warning look that indicated the woman pressed against him. He wasn't in the mood for mourning mothers, or women who just wanted to hold a firm-bodied man.

Mikhail did look very fine, rawly masculine, grim, uncomfortable and in need of rescuing.

Ellie shook her head and grinned, enjoying the situation of Mikhail asking her for help. He was on his own. Or she could save him for a price....

"I was just telling Mrs. Hightower how the reception can be held near the pool, if she likes—"

Mikhail frowned at Ellie. He had given her strict orders that there would be no wedding cake in the Amoteh's pool water, no broken champagne glasses on the tile floors.

Over the head of the sobbing woman who was actually holding him tightly, Mikhail's gaze slowly went down Ellie's body.

Ellie hurried to explain her unusual combination of clothes. "Mrs. Hightower understands that I was working with swimsuits when she arrived—trying to understand the sizing. She said she doesn't mind that I'm dressed like this."

Those sea-green eyes darkened, taking in the gray suit jacket over her midnight blue maillot bathing suit and the triangular pareo tied at her hips, the fringes brushing her legs. He stared at her feet in the flip-flops and then slowly repeated his journey upward to her lips. The sensual heat inside Ellie rose immediately; she could almost feel him holding her, within her—*linked*.... More than their bodies had touched, and that brief moment had terrified her.

For a brief moment, Ellie knew that he wanted to pick her up and carry her away. The gesture would be primitive, possessive and pure Mikhail. The impact of his raw sensuality took away her breath and warmed her body, quivering along her skin as though his lips were skimming—

Not that she was a passive partner in his arms. Mikhail called forth a certain savagery within her, the need to claim him....

Locked in Mikhail's dark sensual stare, her blood heated, pounded through her. She ached for the touch of his hands, for his lips, for his breath curling over her skin.

But more than that, she ached for the sense that with him, she was finally home.

She struggled back to the business matter at hand. "Of course, the reception will close the pool to guests at that time of year, so there will be an extra charge."

Mrs. Hightower nuzzled Mikhail's chest and he saw that he was at Ellie's mercy. She had picked the perfect time for blackmail. "I see no problem with that," he said as lightly as his frustration would allow.

Ellie beamed and reached for Mrs. Hightower, easing her away. The woman was still reaching for Mikhail as Ellie stood in front of him. She wrapped her arm around Mrs. Hightower's shoulders and guided her away from Mikhail.

"Let me show you the rooms, Mrs. Hightower. I'm certain the wedding party will be well pleased. We're having several weddings this summer and each one will be very special. Amoteh has a lovely little white church, or you might want to use our facilities for the wedding. Our ballroom is equipped to hold a really big crowd, but we do have manicured gardens and an outside ceremony would be lovely."

Relieved that the woman was moving away from him, Mikhail slapped the file he had been holding against his thigh. Ellie's flurry of proposals included those tennis and golf pros that he had already refused.

But then, thinking was difficult when Ellie's shapely backside was swaying elegantly, the fringe a seduction. He could almost feel those slender feet smoothing his calves as her legs cradled his body, moving against him. He could almost hear those soft little cries, taste her—

Mikhail realized that Jarek was standing beside him. "So is everything working out with Ellie?" Jarek asked lightly.

"Mmm. She's sweet really. Very skilled at handling difficult situations. Smart...smells like wildflowers, soft— she's got the cutest little girl smile when she's trying to get her way...." Mikhail turned to see Jarek's wide grin. Mikhail had done his share of teasing Jarek as he pursued Leigh and now it was his brother's turn to repay the favor. "Lay off."

"Did she tell you about her plans to start marketing Stepanov lemon oil polish? Mom and Ellie were working on the promotion earlier. Get ready for a furniture oil sampler to be added to the Amoteh's bath and body products."

Mikhail groaned and left in the wake of his brother's roaring laughter.

"A stone path would be more picturesque for weddings than the heavy timber walkway in the garden. And a koi pond is a must. You could use the coins thrown in it for wishes for a charity." Ellie braced herself against the wind sweeping over the golf course as she argued with Mikhail three days later.

The wind riffled through his hair as he scowled down at her. "More pool cleaning bills."

"Super-size goldfish and good fortune, Mikhail. No outdoor wedding is complete without a stone walkway, a rose garden, a trellis for portraits and a goldfish pond."

Locked in his budget and manager mode, Mikhail was never more tempting, a real challenge to get to the passionate man beneath, Ellie thought. Because she had to tease him, she batted her lashes and cooed, "You know I'm right, Mikie."

Mikhail's snort said he differed, but there was that dark gleam in his eyes that said he enjoyed the slight flirtation. "You're enjoying yourself, aren't you?"

She felt strong and good and fiercely clean. "Immensely."

"Good."

The sunlight tangled between them as Mikhail reached to smooth the windblown strand from her cheek. "That's good," he repeated quietly, gently. "You're good at what you do—smoothing potential wrinkles, working with difficult wedding planners, organizing social dinners and events. That's what you did, wasn't it? Moved in to soothe whatever friction Paul created with his bullying? You picked up, delivered and eased any tension in his business and his private relationships. You were the linchpin in your family, moving between Paul and Hillary. Always Hillary. This must be terribly difficult for you, fighting a sister you raised and one that you still love."

Ellie swallowed tightly as a myriad of bitter memories swept through the pine-scented wind. "Paul paid me well. I arranged his parties, chauffeured and entertained his business associates, and he paid me. You know him, Mikhail. It was business, not that I was his beloved daughter."

"You could have left at any time, but you didn't—because you loved Hillary."

"She was ten years younger. Her mother left immediately after her birth. Of course I loved her."

"Of course," Mikhail agreed softly. "I have friends in Paul's business circle, and I made a few calls to see why someone as good as you would have ruined a business deal that was almost cinched. You're far too good to let go of prime information at a cocktail party that could possibly botch a big real estate deal. Hillary was tipsy at the party and angry with Paul. She deliberately found the potential seller and told him that after the property was purchased, Paul was going to sell off what he didn't need at a multi-million-dollar profit. You covered for her, didn't you? In that time and in others, so that Paul wouldn't disinherit her. You knew he needed you to cover for him, glossing over his roughshod techniques, so you stepped in to protect Hillary. But when Tanya came, you knew that you had to act."

Ellie fought tears, tangled by the painful past. "I'd rather not replay this whole mess, Mikhail."

He took her hand to his face, pressing it there with his own calloused one. "Know that I care. Know that I am here."

Mikhail stood in the Stepanov showroom, watching the women in the parking lot below. He cuddled the infant in his arms and kissed Katerina's curls. "If your father wasn't in the kitchen, wooing Georgia into making a surprise dinner for your mother, I'd be down there with Ellie."

But as a very private man who locked his past away, he knew that Ellie might not want him at her side. Mikhail rocked Katerina against him, and admired the woman he loved. "Of course I love her. Of course, Katerina. But we are in a storm, and she fears for her child. Now is not the right time."

While Paul hadn't made his move, Hillary had arrived in a bright red SUV with a heavily muscled woman in a sweat suit.

Clearly arguing, Hillary's expression was hard and fierce,

while Ellie's pale face was rigid, her hair flying around her. The diamonds on Hillary's hand flashed in the sunlight as she slapped Ellie's face, and the muscular woman moved in to hold Ellie's arms.

Mikhail was on the move immediately, easing Katerina into Jarek's arms as he passed. Jarek skillfully placed the infant into the soft carrying sack in front of him, tucking her blankets around her. He held her close, protectively, a father comfortable with nurturing his child.

"Call the folks," Mikhail said. "Tell them to keep Tanya inside and I would appreciate you being there, too."

"Done," Jarek said firmly, and checked Katerina's blankets before leaving the resort.

Outside, Mikhail moved quickly toward the scene where Hillary was screeching, "Where is she? You tell me right now, Ellie. I'm taking her."

The sisters were alike in appearance, but Hillary's harsh lifestyle showed in the bitterness of her mouth, in the glitter of her heavily mascaraed eyes. The smell of alcohol bit into the fresh salt air as she turned toward Mikhail, who was quickly walking toward them. "You. Daddy will take care of you. He's making plans, so you'd better give me my daughter right now."

Mikhail fought the fury inside him and stared at the woman holding Ellie. She frowned and slowly released Ellie. "We came for the girl," she said.

He placed his arm around Ellie and she shrugged him away, her eyes lashing at him. "I can handle this."

There was blood on her cheek, a tiny slash from Hillary's ring as she turned back to her sister. "I'm working here, Hillary. I needed a job and I have one. Tanya is well and happy. That's all there is to it."

"I always knew you two had a thing for each other. I never understood it, but I knew that it was there by the way you kept digging at him. Now you're using him and he's going to lose his precious resort. Daddy said so. Or maybe he's using you. Maybe he's just the same as dear old Dad and needs you to make him look good. That's what Daddy thought—that you made him look good...because you were classy and I wasn't. He wasn't proud of me. He didn't want me around until now that I've got a chance to bring in a man with money and power.... And Tanya is going to cinch the deal for us.... I need a drink. Come on, Freddie—''

Mikhail blocked Hillary's path toward the Amoteh. ''No.''

She pointed to the sprawling resort. ''Dad owns that, you know. I get free Mignon International accommodations wherever I go, and free drinks.''

''Not here, you don't. Consider the Amoteh and grounds off-limits.'' Mikhail caught the open hand Hillary sailed at him. ''You may leave now.''

''You'll be sorry...both of you,'' Hillary shot at Ellie as she climbed into the SUV. She slammed the door and roared out of the parking lot, headed for Amoteh.

''There you have it,'' Ellie said quietly. ''Family loving time, Lathrop style. I've got to see about Tanya.''

''She's at my parents and Jarek knows that Hillary is around. She's safe, Ellie.''

She was shaking and pale, as she watched the SUV drive toward a local tavern and pull into the Seagull's Perch parking lot. ''It's good she's got someone with her. She needs someone to take care of her. When Hillary hurts or she's mad, she drinks.''

Love and the frustration wrapped in her quiet words. Mikhail caught her chin and turned her cheek for his inspection. ''You're bleeding.''

''Leave me alone,'' Ellie ordered bitterly as her hand pushed his away. ''Don't touch me.''

Mikhail stilled, feeling as though a sheet of ice had slid between them. Locked in the past moments, Ellie did not turn to him, did not let him comfort her. She stood shaking and in pain and she didn't want him to touch her, this woman he adored, whose smile filled him with pleasure, whose tears made him ache.

Her eyes held him, soft and damp with pain she could not release, her lips trembling and vulnerable. The past held her, cold and bitter, and he was helpless against it.

"I have to go to my daughter," she whispered desperately as she began moving toward the wooded path leading to the Stepanovs. "I have to know that she is safe."

Mikhail stood in the cold wind, watching Ellie run over the path. *In her pain, she had not turned to him....*

Seven

That night, after Tanya was asleep, Mikhail knocked on the door to Ellie's suite. When she opened it, he towered over her, his expression grim. His white dress shirt hung open, and his hair was rumpled as if he had been running his fingers through it.

"Let me see your face," he ordered, framing her chin between his thumb and finger and tilting it to the light. A fierce hot wave of unspoken anger hit her as his eyes glittered, green as emeralds.

"I'm not hurt." She stood rigid, unused to a caring touch.

"How many times have you been hurt and no one took care of you?" he demanded roughly as his thumb smoothed the small injury.

Memories of past pain flashed by Ellie as she closed her eyes to him. Her pride was slipping away, humbled by his attention. "I'm not a victim. I never have been. The only thing that matters in this is Tanya's safety."

"Of course," he said more gently as he smoothed her cheek. She was beginning to understand that his big hands conveyed his emotions better than his words. When he cherished and enjoyed any of the craftsmen's work, a flower, or a child, his fingertips traced and his eyes followed the flow. Now he had focused on her, his touch gentle, explorative.

"Mikhail?"

"What?" His deep voice was uneven and harsh and she knew what he needed, to hold her and to protect her. She sensed him waiting to be asked.

When her lips moved and the words she wanted didn't come, Mikhail's expression tightened, a shadow crossing the stark masculine planes. He nodded and closed the door between them.

After a sleepless night, endlessly replaying Hillary's bitterness, the fear that Tanya would be taken, and haunted by the pain in Mikhail's expression, as if he'd taken a slap, Ellie braced herself to face him.

At eight o'clock in the morning, Mikhail was unapproachable—cool, crisp and businesslike, a man of steel, and not the lover she had known. While going over schedules and plans in his office, Ellie attempted to break through that veneer. "I'm sorry that I involved you in this, Mikhail."

His angular face was all shadows and planes, a muscle contracting in his jaw as he slashed a signature across papers. She ached to smooth the slight shaving cut on his cheek.

Was he regretting making love with her?

Those dark green eyes pinned her and Mikhail leaned back in his chair, studying her. He tossed his pen onto the papers. "Anything else?"

There was so much she wanted to say, but Mikhail's expression wasn't encouraging. Just below the cool surface, he was simmering with anger. "I...no, thank you."

The muscle in his cheek contracted and his lips tight-

ened. He picked up the pen and began studying the paperwork on his desk, clearly dismissing her. "Then we both
have work to do, don't we?"

As Ellie walked with Tanya on the beach later that day,
her mind was on Hillary's violence and Mikhail.

Mikhail's head had gone back as if taking a slap when
she'd said, "Don't touch me." *She'd hurt him.*

She was ashamed of what he had just seen, of Hillary,
the little sister she had always tried to protect, drunk and
abusive. It wasn't easy for Ellie to blend her life with Mikhail's, to understand that he needed to protect her. A sensitive, emotional man beneath his steel exterior, Mikhail as
a person with needs and unexpected vulnerability was new
to her.

On the beach, sandpipers scurried in a zigzag line and
waves tipped by foam caressed the sand. Seaweed, dark
green against the brown sand, shifted almost sensually with
the kiss of the water.

Ellie inhaled the salt scent into her, listening to the gulls,
and she should have felt a measure of peace—she didn't.
She felt as if Chief Kamakani's curse still prowled the land
he hated, and danger lurked nearby. Ellie briefly scanned
the shore and the pier and higher on a boardwalk, near the
piers lashed together with cable, a big man stood—Lars.

Poised against the blue sky, he seemed to be watching
Tanya. Lars had already proven to be a dangerous man,
and only a few people were on the beach in the late afternoon. Ellie hurried Tanya up the rough wooden steps to
Amoteh's tourist street, where there were more people.
Filled with artists' seascapes and colorful bouquets of stat-
ice and wind chimes made from seashells, the shops were
still open and Tanya was delighted to enter the toy store.

Caught up in the little girl's excitement over a miniature
tea set, Ellie forgot about Lars and enjoyed the cluttered
store. The owners, elderly sisters, chatted about weather
and toys and Ellie purchased a small teddy bear for Tanya.

The sisters were still chatting happily as Ellie left the store, Tanya holding her hand.

The cheerful sisters eased Ellie's tension, and she forgot about Lars as she stopped to talk with Lisa Peterson, a maid at the Amoteh. She'd just bought material for her daughters' Easter dresses, and missing her own sewing, Ellie admired the delicate rosebuds on the fabric.

One glance told her that Tanya was gone and fear electrified Ellie. Hillary wasn't above kidnaping.... "Tanya!"

From two stores down the street, Tanya answered immediately. "Mommy!"

Hurrying toward the sound, Ellie's heart froze as she saw Lars holding Tanya, a lollipop in the little girl's hand. "Put her down," Ellie ordered fiercely.

"He's going to show me some puppies, Mommy, but I said I'd have to ask you first," Tanya said as Lars seemed to debate releasing the child.

Every nerve in Ellie's body prickled as Lars's expression changed to defiance.

"Put her down now," Ellie ordered again, surprised that she could sound so cool and firm when fear and temper were raging inside her.

Lars's small eyes narrowed as he glanced around the street to find several people watching them. He lowered Tanya to the ground, none too gently. "You're pretty small to be ordering a man around, but then I ain't no Mikhail Stepanov either to let a woman run my life, Ms. Lathrop of the fancy, la-di-da money. You're the same as any other woman, and don't you forget it."

"Leave us alone," Ellie said quietly, fiercely.

Lars leered down at her, and her anger vibrated, almost throwing her against him. "Well, now. Stepanov's woman has a temper, don't she? I'll bet you're a real she-cat—"

"That's enough."

Lars glanced around once more as if considering his options, and then shrugged. "We ain't done, lady," he said before walking away.

Ellie shook as she knelt to gather Tanya into her arms, and to throw away the lollipop. "Don't you ever, ever go with that man again, or take anything he gives you."

When Tanya blinked and tears came to her eyes, Ellie regretted showing her fear. She hugged Tanya close, and looked up to see Lars watching them over his shoulder. "I'll get you candy, Tanya, but never take any from someone you don't know."

"He said he knew you."

"Well, he does, but he isn't a man I like," Ellie stated fiercely.

Rita, the waitress at the Seagull's Perch, stopped and studied Ellie. "Everything all right? I saw Lars talking with your little girl. You look just like your sister, Ellie—she was talking to Lars at the Seagull. I wouldn't trust him if I were you. He's had a longtime grudge against the Stepanovs, and it's no secret that—"

Rita glanced warily at Tanya, who was watching with wide eyes. "Mikhail isn't just playing games, Ellie."

"Mikhail plays games," Tanya stated adamantly. "He plays with me."

Ellie held Tanya on her hip, still caught in the fear of seeing Lars holding her. Hillary was capable of anything to get her way, and she'd been talking to Lars.... "Did you hear what they said, my sister and Lars?"

"Only that she'd make it worth his while. Did I say something wrong? You just went white."

Ellie was already moving up the wooden steps to the Amoteh, hurrying Tanya along. Then Mikhail stood in front of her, and Tanya ran ahead to him. "Mikhail! I got a new teddy bear at the toy store."

He lifted her into his arms and kissed her cheek, but his eyes held Ellie's. "What's wrong with Mommy, Tanya?"

Tanya looped an arm around his neck and looked solemnly at Ellie. "She's mad at me for talking to the man. I just wanted the sucker. She threw it away."

"Lars," Ellie said quietly. "I probably overreacted. He's talked to my sister."

"I know. Henry, the bartender, called me." Mikhail kissed Tanya again, but his eyes never left Ellie. They agreed silently that Hillary would use the resources at hand, and Lars had added a potential new dangerous dimension. "Let's go inside and you can tell me what you saw in the store, okay? You know what?" Mikhail asked Tanya. "I have a sucker in my office shaped like a strawberry just for you. Then I have a meeting to attend, and Grandma Mary Jo wants you to come to dinner."

An hour and a half later, Mikhail came to dinner at the Stepanovs'. He wore a taut, brooding look. His knuckles on his right hand were bruised, proving to Ellie he had met Lars. When she looked at his hand, Mikhail shrugged and spoke quietly. "It's what he understands. I think it would be wise for Tanya to visit Mother's family in Texas. She was planning a trip anyway. Paul is coming in a few days. He won't be sweet."

Over dinner, the month-long trip to Mary Jo's family in Texas was quickly arranged, while Fadey would stay and meet the rising orders for Stepanov furniture. Since Tanya already had her favorite doll and her day-bag of clothing with her, whatever else she needed would be purchased.

The Stepanovs carefully avoided commenting about the scratch on Ellie's cheek, though Fadey had caught her chin and turned the injury to his inspection. He kissed the small wound. "There. Get better, little one. You let my Mikhail care for you, eh? He's a good boy, you know."

She'd managed a wobbly smile, because Mikhail had looked so fierce and angry with her.

Delighted with the tiny teacups and saucers that Mikhail had purchased from the sisters, Tanya bubbled with excitement. She carefully served water from the tiny teapot into the cups.

"Delicious," Fadey exclaimed as he watched Mikhail stare at Ellie, and her blush rise.

Her hand shook as she lifted the tiny tea cup to her lips and avoided Mikhail's dark, searing look. *Don't touch me,* she'd said and hurt him, a man who needed to comfort and to hold her.

A graceful woman, sensing tension and skilled at soothing her family, Mary Jo smiled at Ellie, who was now holding a sleepy Tanya. "Well, Tanya, darlin', if we're going to get up early to see all those cows and horses, then we'd better get going— Come on, Mama. You both should stay the night here if we're getting an early start. Tuck your little girl in. Goodness, you don't look like more than a girl yourself."

Ellie cradled Tanya as she slid into sleep, and then lay quietly, listening to Mikhail and his parents talk in the living room.

In her world, tender emotions weren't exposed. Worn by her scene with Hillary and fear for Tanya, Ellie regretted not taking what Mikhail offered, the comfort of his arms. How badly she'd wanted to step into his arms…but the past had tangled around her. Giving herself into someone else's care seemed like a bridge she couldn't cross easily. Too exhausted, she slid into sleep, holding Tanya close….

She awoke to see Mikhail outlined in the doorway, and then the door closed, just as he had shut her away from him.

Ellie gathered Tanya closer, nuzzled the girl's fragrant hair, and ached for Mikhail's arms around her.

Mikhail tossed the telephone records onto Ellie's desk. "Paul and Hillary have been calling, and you didn't see fit to tell me."

Her office was small and cluttered and feminine, splashed with color and daffodils, and he felt like a barbarian striking out at her. In the two days since Tanya and his mother had gone, Ellie had withdrawn from him, her eyes shadowed as she worked long hours trying to prove herself. The telephone records said she had made several calls to her family, and their calls had been erratic. Whatever was going on between them, she'd cut him out....

He had given his heart to her, and she didn't trust him.

"You've been busy," Ellie said evenly.

"Yes, of course. I always am at this time of year."

"I mean that you're taking time to check on me. It's private, Mikhail. More threats, more anger. Typical Lathrop stuff. I'll deal with it. And don't you ever fight with Lars again. There are other ways of handling him."

Mikhail thought of the scene in the Seagull's Perch—Lars had swung first, and Mikhail had finished the bulkier man easily. Lars wouldn't admit to anything, nor was he a man to take a warning; he made no pretenses—he hated the Stepanovs.

"The situation with Lars is old and bitter and not of your making.... You said, 'I'll deal with it,' not *'We'll* deal with it.'"

"I just don't want you or your family hurt. Hillary is one thing, but you know Paul. He's playing the waiting game. He's offered me a job."

She was leaving. His body tensed as though taking a blow. "And?"

"If I leave you now, there's no one to cover my plans, to follow them through."

How could she leave him? Mikhail fought anger and pain. "Don't let that stop you. We'll handle it."

"You're angry."

"Yes. But that doesn't change this—" He reached to tug her up into his arms, and in his frustration took her lips in heat and hunger. She gasped once, tensed to resist, and then her hands were in his hair, holding him as he wanted.

Aware of her body softening into his, Mikhail broke the kiss and studied Ellie's drowsy eyes, her swollen lips. He ran his hands down her body and then back up, releasing her quickly. "So it was always there for us. Just this, if no more. Have a nice day."

Ellie's expression darkened. "You, too, Mikie. And by the way, Lars isn't your problem. He's mine. I'll talk to him about Hillary."

Ellie had no conception of how brutal Lars could be—he'd abused his wife and son. "No, you won't. Leave Lars to me."

Her head tilted and the strands of honey blond swirled along her cheek. "I've been managing without you for quite a while."

"We both know that you need me. That's why you're here, isn't it? Because you need me?"

Ellie did need him, at least on one level, but did she want him on a deeper one?

"I don't suppose you need me."

He needed her physically and in ways that were new to him, but he wouldn't admit it, not now. His body aching, he smiled tightly at the taunt and walked from her office.

He paused when something soft and fragrant hit his back. He picked up a daffodil from the scattered bouquet on the carpet, broke off the stem and stuck the flower in his lapel. "Thank you so much."

Five long hours later, in front of Jarek's oceanside cabin, Mikhail sat looking out into the night, the moonlight trailing over the water to him. His emotions swirled around him like a storm. The need for Ellie was more than a physical one, it was one of the heart, and he was pushing, wanting her....

A sound told him he wasn't alone and then he caught Ellie's fresh scent. "Mikhail?"

He didn't want her to see him now, to know how deeply he hurt. *She didn't trust him.* "Don't touch me. If you do, I won't be responsible."

She eased onto the worn beach towel beside him. "You're always responsible. You've done so much for everyone."

Don't touch me. That was what Ellie had said after arguing with Hillary. He knew now how Ellie felt, as if one touch would shatter her control.

The moonlight settled, silvery upon her hair, the slight breeze lifting, toying with the silky strands. She was wearing his brown leather jacket with her jeans and that pleased him. "I'm wearing this because I miss you, Mikhail. It feels like you and you've been so distant. I know I hurt you.... I didn't mean to, but... Is there someone else?"

As if he could hold anyone else, share his body and his life with another woman. He looked down at her. "You could ask that?"

In the moonlight, her blush rose to fascinate him.

Ellie looked out at the ocean and her hand trembled as she smoothed her hair, a very good sign—but then, when a man is desperate for a sign that he affects a woman...

"You are a potent, attractive man, Mikhail. Very potent. It's difficult to think around you, especially when you turn on the charm."

Well, he thought, that compliment did help. "So I have charm."

"Just a bit. It's rough and edgy and stormy, but charm, just the same. Don't let that fact go to your head."

"And I make you nervous. Why?"

"Because you can be very difficult when you want, and you know good and well that I've come to apologize. You're making me grovel, Mikie, and I really wouldn't advise that. You came bristling into my office today, attacked me, and kissed me to prove your point—okay, I'm susceptible to you—and then you walked off. You're cocky and arrogant, and I don't know why I want you, but I do."

"Ah, just that touch of anger. So I've gotten to you, have I?"

Her eyes were silver in the night, burning him. "You know you do. You always have since I met you years ago."

Proof that she cared would help, Mikhail thought as he

lay back, his hands behind his head, waiting…. "Convince me."

"Ohhh!" Ellie threw herself over him, holding his wrists with her hands. "You're so irritating. You know just how to set me off."

He moved slightly, enjoying the feel of her curves over him and allowed his pleased smirk to wrap around one word: "Sometimes."

She stared down at him and blinked.

"I love it when you think, darling," he said, enjoying her expressions.

"I am thinking that sometimes I set you off, Mikie," she challenged.

This time, Mikhail didn't hide his grin. With Ellie, he felt young and impetuous and certain. "Of course."

Ellie's smile stopped his thoughts, and he waited, enjoying the moment and wondering what she would do next. "You can have me, if you want," he offered softly.

She tapped his lips lightly with her fingertip. "But then, you would have me, wouldn't you? That's generally how it works."

"With us—yes."

Sadness lurked in Ellie's expression as her hand smoothed his cheek, her eyes searching his face, and he wondered if she understood how another woman hadn't wanted him, how much that had hurt….

He needed this, Mikhail thought as Ellie dived in to prove her point, kissing him hungrily, her mouth open and hot upon his. There would be tender moments, but now he needed the fire between them to burn away any doubt of how he felt.

Mikhail eased Ellie away and stood, hurrying to scoop her up into his arms. "I've been staying here," he whispered as he carried her up the steps. "I could not sleep so close to you and not want you."

Without her, anywhere, he ached to touch her, to hold her, to see her. He'd never been lonely before, always pushing himself, immersed in work, but Ellie had changed his life, enriched the fabric, his senses. The nights were endless, haunting him with her scent, the sounds of her passion, the sheets raw against his skin when he would have her body touching his. Was it the same for her? Did she ache for him as much?

Did he give her what she needed most?

"Mikhail, hurry...." She snuggled against him, her arms tight around his shoulders as he carried her into Jarek's simple cabin.

Mikhail placed her on her feet. He reached for a small box on the table and opened it. "For you."

He lifted his hand to smooth her hair from her cheek. "I want you to wear these and think of me. That you are not alone anymore, that you have me."

Inside the box gleamed elegant feminine earrings, a lacy length of gold with beads of rose quartz and drops of moonstone. In Mikhail's big, dark hands, they seemed alive, so fragile, as intricate as the woman he loved. "My grandmother's," he said quietly. "It would please me if you accepted them."

Ellie stroked them with her finger. "They're lovely, but I couldn't. They belong to your family."

"No other woman has worn them, and it's time. This is how I see you, soft and feminine, yet with strength and love." Mikhail took her hand and lifted it to his lips, pressing his lips into her palm. "Take them. Take me."

Would she have him? Would she trust him? Would she...?

Mikhail caught his breath as Ellie's soft cry echoed in the spartan room, her arms circling his neck. The impact of her body thrown against him sent him backward and tumbling into the big solid Stepanov bed.

Heads resting on the same pillow, they stared at each other and Ellie ran her fingers through his hair, studying him. "You oversimplify, Stepanov."

"You complicate."

Ellie's hand smoothed his face, his hair. "Let me up."

He inhaled roughly. She chose to leave him, to retreat. Ellie eased from the bed to walk around the simply furnished room, touching the good sturdy furniture, noting the tiny kitchenette, the basic bathroom. "Was she here?"

"My ex-wife? No." Mikhail thought of the luxurious home JoAnna had demanded. Stark and furnished with cold furniture and marble, it now belonged to someone else.

"Was she in your suite, your apartment at the Amoteh?"

"Yes. But not as my wife. We were divorced by that time." JoAnna's big plans hadn't materialized as she'd wished and she'd come back for more money. She'd failed to seduce him and had ripped into him, accusing him of ruining their marriage.

"I went into your apartment, missing you. I can feel her there, Mikhail. You loved her. You were still aching years ago when I came to the Amoteh's opening. You'd been divorced a year then and still brooding. I was so angry with you for letting her hurt you. Even then, I wanted to tear her away from you. And I was angry at you for showing no emotions whatsoever. Now I know how much you ached."

He sensed that Ellie was picking her moment, making her decision, and he could only wait and hope. Then, in the next moment, his emotions carried him to his feet and he paced the length of the cabin, sorting out the past for Ellie as he had for no one else. "I thought I loved her. I changed, not her. JoAnna needed more than I could give her. I…didn't satisfy her."

That was the first time he'd made such an admission aloud, but it was important that Ellie know.

She opened her hand, and the earrings tumbled onto the small table. Would she refuse him, what they could have?

The tiny jingle of gold caused his heart to chill. Was Ellie discarding what ran sometimes hot and feverish and other times gentle between them?

Mikhail forced himself to go on, to finish what he had begun, to give Ellie the truth that had gnawed at him for years. He stared out of the window, the continuous flow of waves as they had been through the years. "We had grand plans—a resort chain of our own. I wanted it as badly as she—money, prestige, world travel.... Then I changed, I saw what I could do here, to help Amoteh, and then I knew JoAnna wouldn't be happy here, I took the job Paul offered—a trade-off to manage a top resort, set in Amoteh. JoAnna was furious, and I thought a house would settle her—and a baby. She took the house, which was more than we could afford, but rejected my child. Then I learned that she only became pregnant to use my child as leverage to get what she wanted. I changed," he repeated. "I wanted more."

"For those you love," Ellie said softly.

"I should have been— We grew apart, and when I looked back, I saw that the intimacy wasn't there, the friendship and the respect and the sharing. We were separate people."

Mikhail smiled briefly, contrasting his description of his relationship with JoAnna with how complete he felt with Ellie. "We were 'unlinked.' I come here sometimes to get away from what could have been, what I could have done, the mistakes I made, the reasons our marriage failed."

"I like this place better," Ellie said firmly as she removed his leather jacket and hung it over the back of a chair. "And I like wearing your clothes. Do you mind?"

He leaned back against the kitchenette counter, crossing his arms so that he wouldn't reach out for her. "Yes, now I do. I mind you wearing clothes of any kind."

She nodded and kicked off her sneakers. Ellie slowly, thoughtfully bent to place them beside his boots. Then, with those same careful movements, as though she were making an important decision, working her way through to the final solution, she eased away her long-sleeve sweater and folded it neatly, placing it on the table. "I like this place. With you."

In the moonlight sliding through the windows, she was silvery soft curves, graceful as she slid from her jeans and folded them neatly, too. It was a feminine ceremony, Mikhail realized, and one that was slowly killing him.

He couldn't move, every muscle tense as Ellie picked up the earrings and studied them before sliding them into her lobes. The movement fascinated him; Mikhail had never seen such grace, the shift of her body, the silvery lights of her hair sliding around her face.

She walked slowly toward him, her face in shadow, but the gold gleaming softly as it swayed seductively amid her hair. Moonlight caught the tilt of her breasts, the rounded curve of her hips, the darker shadows between her thighs—

When she stood close, the scent of her skin beckoning, Mikhail couldn't speak; he could only put out his hand to stroke her thigh, to trail his fingers along her hip. She quivered at his touch. Then her hand was in his, soft and feminine and yet strong as he brought it to his lips.

"You're wearing too many clothes, Mikie," Ellie whispered.

As he undressed, she touched him softly on his shoulders, the muscle of his arm, on his hip, winnowing her fingers through the hair on his chest. Each touch, each look aroused, until his blood pounded and heated and knew....

"So here we are," she whispered as he eased her body close to his, the curve and flow of man and woman, so near and yet not one.

This was the mating, he thought as he cupped her breasts, cherished them with his lips, savoring the taste, the feminine scent of her skin. Her sigh took his desire higher, his body taut and aching, and yet he was determined to give her everything as he eased her onto the bed, covering her with his body.

She opened to him, easing to take him tightly, slowly, within her, and Mikhail fought release, his body humming for it. Half-closed, silvery in the night, Ellie's eyes watched him, her cheeks flushed, her lips moist, the earrings gleaming amid the tousled silky strands. She was magic and desire; she was his, the woman who was the other part of him, who was his life.

She was mysterious, waiting, hot, holding her secrets, beckoning him on with the flow of her hips and her breasts nudging his chest, her stomach supple and undulating, those long legs trapping him, her hands caressing....

The storm came too quickly, a flurry of passion and heat and cries that pulsed around them, in them, as Mikhail met her there, fought to hold her, a primitive claiming driven by her sounds, her mouth on his flesh, her hands roaming his back—

They fought on that plane, no gentle taking for either of them, each burning into the other, forging a new level to their relationship, raw and clean and true.

Mikhail felt her body tense as his own tore from his control, and then the world spiraled around them, twisted and made them one....

With his face against her throat, he could feel her pulse slow and treasured what she had given—what she had taken—as her hands soothed and caressed in the aftermath of their passion.

She was complete.

Ellie gave herself to the peace only Mikhail could bring her, and then he began to move again, rising above her, fierce and demanding, and she would have no less....

He eased the hair from her cheek, her ear, and in the moonlight his expression was primitive, all glittering eyes and hard planes. She knew what pleased him, that she wore his mark, that she was his, and she reveled in that, because she held him within her and reminded him by clenching her body.

She met his dark look, challenged him, enjoying the seduction of this man, this wonderful, exciting man, this warrior, making her feel like a woman, to know a woman's heart and strength and hungers....

Mikhail pressed his hot, hard face against the spot between her throat and her ear and his hands caressed her, and suddenly her body flew into the storm again, the hunger renewed.

In the night, she heard Mikhail chuckle as she moved over him, taking what she wanted, taking his lips, tasting him, becoming one again.

In the dawn, she awoke to Mikhail sliding from her arms and legs; he padded to the bathroom and when she heard the shower running, Ellie held his pillow tight, caught his scent and slid back into sleep. When she awoke the second time, Mikhail was lying beside her, toying with her hair, the earrings.

"Breakfast?" He had shaved, and the laughter in his expression caused her to smile.

She could have loved him again, if she could move. "You know I want you, not food."

His kiss was brief, playful. "I know. I am sexy. You want me. You adore me," he drawled.

The statement was so unlike Mikhail that she had to laugh, and then Mikhail was studying her. He turned her cheek and frowned at her throat. "I was afraid of that—I didn't take time to shave last night. You're scratched here." His finger explored her throat.

"Kiss it and make it well," she challenged, feeling very certain of herself.

But Mikhail had his own agenda. He eased the blankets away from her body, studying the length as his hand moved over her, his expression dark and intent. "You gave yourself to me."

"Correction— You gave yourself to me, several times." Still shy of Mikhail, Ellie fought drawing up the blankets to shield herself.

Mikhail smiled gently. "Nervous?"

"You're very intense."

Mikhail touched her breasts, a fingertip playing with her nipple until she pressed his hand close with hers. ''Come here,'' she ordered breathlessly, reaching for him.

When Mikhail grinned, a devastating flash of white teeth against his tanned skin, Ellie decided to tease him. ''Or we could have that breakfast.''

Mikhail reacted just as she wanted. ''Breakfast can wait.''

Later, they sat on the porch—Ellie on Mikhail's lap—watching the morning come to life—seagulls swooping to strut on the beach, sandpipers scurrying, old Boyd Jones out with his bucket, picking up clutter that had been left by irresponsible picnickers, Mario Ferguson jogging with his earphones.

''I needed this,'' Ellie said as Mikhail tucked a blanket closer around her. ''It's been so long since I relaxed that I feel like I'm coming apart.''

He kissed her forehead and, beneath the blanket, caressed her breasts, clothed only in his T-shirt and his leather jacket. ''You come apart beautifully.''

''Mmm.'' She snuggled against him, resting her head on his chest. She couldn't resist wiggling her hips against him, and through the denim layers between them found him responding, hardening once more.

''Let's make a day of it, shall we?'' Mikhail asked as he toyed with her earring, blowing gently into her ear. ''Take some time off?''

''Can't. I've got a meeting with ten wedding planners this morning.''

His disapproving growl was long and low and hungry as he nuzzled her throat.

Ellie couldn't help laughing as he nuzzled that spot behind her ear and growled. Mikhail in a playful mood wasn't to be missed. ''I just rescheduled,'' she told him, and this time his growl was one of sheer agreement.

Eight

Ellie smiled as she hurried up the steps of the small cabin and flicked the wind chimes Bliss had made from spoons; they spun and tinkled in the first of April sunlight. She balanced the grocery sack in one arm as she opened the door, and when it closed behind her, she placed the sack on the table and removed her light jacket.

It was such a good place, just for her and Mikhail. Ellie stroked Mikhail's flannel shirt hung by the door, drawing it to her face, inhaling his scent. In the shadowy silence she heard his chuckle again as he tickled her on their bed. Yes, it was a very good place.

With one touch, the big Stepanov rocking chair that Mikhail had brought to the cabin creaked gently, moving back and forth. He'd said that Tanya was not too big to be cuddled and rocked, and with a boyish grin added that he wanted to rock Ellie, too.

She'd lived in penthouses and mansions and rented rooms, but if ever she'd had a first home filled with love and safety, this small cabin was it. She'd tried to give those things to Tanya, and yet it was the first time anyone had given them to her. A sense of homecoming warmth surrounded her immediately. Tonight, she would cook dinner for Mikhail—a gesture that was a little old-fashioned for the Ellie Lathrop she'd always been, to serve a man, to tend him.

She smoothed the earrings he had given her. In the past week, each time he saw her wearing them, his expression softened, and a riveting sense of being fresh and new and desired washed over her.

At work, he was all business, but when walking along the pier, holding her hand, Mikhail might smile down at her and then bend for a light, friendly kiss—or he might tug her into a shadowy spot, flatten her against a wall with his body, and then he was her lover, as eager for her as she was for him. On the beach, he was a boy again, teasing her, chasing her, and she was the girl she'd never been, laughing and carefree....

Hurrying to start the spaghetti sauce, Ellie placed Mikhail's old flannel shirt over her blouse and jeans, not only for protection while she cooked, but also because she loved having this token of him near. While the sauce simmered, she swept and cleaned and wished for Mikhail as she showered.

Dressed only in his shirt and her jeans, she dived onto the bed she had shared for two nights with Mikhail. Ellie drew his pillow close to her, nuzzling it and remembering how he had taken one look at her in the bikini she was trying on—okay, she just couldn't resist putting a raincoat over it and hunting him down—just to see his reaction.

When they were alone in the Amoteh's hallway, Mikhail—still distracted by the flurry of women planning a "Boost Your Sexuality" retreat—had frowned down at her. "Women," he had brooded. "I am not going to lecture to them on what a man likes. Or—"

He had been too perfect—unmussed and businesslike

and unlike the man she'd watched shave, and she couldn't resist. "Oh, Mikie…"

He had blinked and looked stunned as she had flashed him, opening her coat.

If she'd been timing his reaction, it might have taken a heartbeat for Mikhail to reach around her, lift her off her feet and, holding her eyes, walk her into a linen closet, which he locked behind him.

"You're going to drive me crazy," he'd said roughly as he pulled the tiny string bow between her breasts.

"Likewise," she had said, arching up into his kiss.

In the shadows, filled with the scent of fresh laundry, Mikhail had grinned and then set about giving her what she wanted.

In the Amoteh's kitchen later, their hands had touched when reaching for a glass and Mikhail had caught hers, bringing her palm to his lips in that tender, humble gesture she adored—but then, she adored the man.

Days and nights of loving Mikhail had made her a little dizzy with happiness. She knew the passion that ran beneath that cool exterior, knew how his body felt against hers, trembling with desire. She knew the dipping curve of his muscular butt, how it felt in her hands, that very cute butt. She knew how his heart beat against hers, how hot his blood pulsed in passion. She knew his tenderness and the peace in his silence.

Was she wrong for wanting a momentary escape, for seeking her own pleasure and happiness, for glimpsing what could be perfect?

Meanwhile Tanya was safe at Mary Jo's family ranch, ecstatic that she would be caring for her own pony and riding it, and feeding chickens and calves.

Ellie frowned slightly as the wind chimes tinkled outside; she almost felt guilty for snatching the happiness Mikhail brought her. She rose to stir the spaghetti sauce, locked in her thoughts. Her momentary peace with Mikhail wouldn't last—Paul hadn't made his move yet, but he would as surely as the tide washed over the shoreline.

Paul. From experience, she knew that he didn't make empty threats, and that he took his time preparing to demolish anyone who he felt had crossed him—and that would be Mikhail.

Hillary. The younger sister who, lacking male affection at an early age, set about gathering men's attention with her woman's body. "She's still my little sister and I love her," Ellie whispered to the shadows.

Outside, Mikhail's surprised shout terrified Ellie. Paul had used "muscle" before to get his way, big thugs who could... Still gripping the wooden spoon, she hurried outside and saw two big men approaching Mikhail on the beach. In denim jackets and jeans, they matched Mikhail for height and build, and reaching him, they began butting him with their shoulders and hooking an arm around his neck. Then, with a shout, the three men went down into the sand, Mikhail on the bottom. The sack he had been carrying broke and groceries spilled upon the sand.

"You let him go!" Running toward the wrestling men, Ellie didn't pause; she threw herself on top of the first man and grabbed his hair, pulling hard. She thumped the man over Mikhail with her spoon. "Get off."

"Hey! That hurt."

"Let him go, or I'll get you again," she threatened fiercely as she pulled the other man's hair.

"Ouch! Lady, let me go."

The whole mass of male muscle beneath her stopped heaving and—and laughing. They were laughing, not arguing and threatening. She peered over the shoulder of the top man down at Mikhail who was grinning at the bottom.

"Hi, honey. Meet my cousins from Wyoming. You're on top of Alexi, and then the other is Danya Stepanov. They're brothers...their father is Viktor, brother to my father."

Sprawled over one man, Ellie hurriedly pushed herself

to her feet. Still worried about him, she stood rigid as the men eased to their feet, and Mikhail stood unharmed and laughing as he hooked an arm around both men's necks.

All three men were rumpled, dusted with sand, and by their strong features, clearly related.

And she could have killed them.

"You were worried for me, yes?" Mikhail asked as she dusted the sand from his hair and clothing—none too gently, because she was thinking of...

He took the spoon from her hand as if fearing she would use it on him.

While she was deciding where to hit him since he'd frightened her so, Mikhail wrapped her in his arms and kissed her long and hard.

He eased her away and looked over her head to the two men. "I love her, of course."

Then, while she was dealing with *I love her, of course,* he bent to ease her over his shoulder and carried her toward the cabin. "Mikhail, let me down."

When he placed her on her feet in the cabin and quickly wrapped his arms around her, Ellie didn't know whether to hit him or kiss him. Alexi and Danya entered the cabin, carrying the groceries. "Hold her. Don't let her go," Alexi warned.

"I love you," Mikhail repeated quietly, solemnly as he smoothed her hair back from her face.

"I love you, too," she whispered unevenly, surprised at the truth, at her ability to say it, returning the emotion with every molecule deep within her.

This time, his kiss was gentle and seeking, and when Ellie opened her eyes, the two big western men were in the kitchenette, their denim jackets hung on the wall. They chopped and stirred as if completely at home and familiar with it.

Mikhail smiled slightly and brought her hand to his lips. "Do you mind?"

Mind what? Loving him, and him loving her?

He eased her onto a chair and bent to towel the sand from her bare feet, warming them with his hands.

"Do I mind what?" *I love you....*

"My cousins dropping in for a visit. They're unmarried and..."

"And you kissed me to show that I was already taken."

He shrugged and stood, his hands on his waist. Mikhail looked down at her as if bracing himself for an argument and he was determined to have his say. "I find I have limitations with you. You are too desirable, especially now with your hair mussed and your color high, those eyes the color of thunderclouds. You look like a woman a man would want to make love to instantly. It was necessary to kiss you. They are Stepanovs. They understand. Are you killing me now, or later?"

Ellie stood and hurried to collect the underwear she wasn't wearing, in anticipation of Mikhail—alone, without his cousins, who were humming what sounded like a Russian folk tune, punctuated with shouts. She slipped into the bathroom and changed with shaking hands. When she had brushed her hair and calmed herself, she braced herself to meet the men. Mikhail's mind shaking, quiet *I love you...*roared over the current male rumble outside the bathroom.

And she'd shocked herself, hearing that she loved him, too!

The men seemed to fill the small cabin and mixed with the scent of her spaghetti sauce was that of beef stroganoff. Alexi was tossing salad greens into a bowl, crumbling feta cheese into it, and Mikhail was setting the table; a fluid mix of English and Russian flowed between them. The men were too potent, too big and overwhelming, Ellie found Danya looking at her. "Sit and have a glass of wine. Tell me about your daughter. Do you have a picture?"

Ellie opened her bag and showed the mini album of Tanya. The ache to hold her daughter curled around her.

"Beautiful. I want children, a lot of them," Danya said quietly. "A Stepanov usually does want children."

His sky-blue eyes locked with hers. One woman hadn't wanted Mikhail's life in Amoteh, or his baby. The Stepanovs were a close family and they worried for each other.

"I want Mikhail," Ellie said quietly, but feared that she could cost him dearly.

Danya's bear hug surprised her, and so did his brief kiss to her cheek. "You're good for him. It's been a long time since we heard him laugh."

"Hey, Ellie," Alexi said as he poured noodles into a bowl. "When dinner is finished, we're going to see Katerina. It's a short stop and then back to Wyoming. We have a lot to do and don't have much time. Are you coming with us, little sister?"

He walked to where she was sitting, struggling with Danya's hug, and bent to lift her to her feet, giving her another hug. Riveted by the open affection, Ellie stood very still in the single room filled with big men, and tried to find her bearings.

"She'll have enough of you, by the time you eat everything," Mikhail said quietly as he came to sit, easing her onto his lap. "Feed me, woman."

Instead, because she needed to react from the big male hugs, she kissed him. "Take that."

The growling noise he made only for her caused her to laugh, because she knew that when alone, they would both be taking—

This was a family, Ellie thought later as the big Stepanov men cuddled and cooed and exclaimed over Jarek and Leigh's baby, delighting in how strong her tiny hand gripped their fingers. Jarek's photographs had captured Katerina's expressions; his love for his wife as she held their daughter seemed to fill their home.

Fadey beamed as he held his granddaughter. "Now I have two, Tanya and Katerina."

When tears came to Ellie's eyes, she turned her face to

Mikhail's shoulder and his arm held her close. He held her hand as the family talked quietly—Viktor loved ranching, but he also missed making furniture with his brothers and the ocean.

Mikhail rocked her against him. "Missing Tanya?"

"Very much."

"It's only for a little while. She's enjoying herself from the sound of it. She called me today. Apparently, there's a pony she'd like to bring home," he said as Bliss passed and patted him on the head. Her color was high and beads of sweat were on her forehead.

Ed was brooding in a corner, a sign that Bliss's midlife moods had changed and she'd zapped him.

"You said you weren't staying long?" she asked Alexi as she served him a large piece of Leigh's double chocolate cake.

"Just overnight and then we'll be on our way. We can't be gone too long from the ranch. Dad needs us."

The men looked at Mikhail, who shook his head as if to stop further explanation.

"So you had a few days off and you came to visit Mikie?" She couldn't help the tease.

Jarek, Alexi and Danya were on Mikhail's nickname instantly. "Oh, Mikie…" they chorused together, grinning at him. "Mikie, Mikie, Mikie."

He groaned and shook his head. "You're going to pay for that," he murmured to Ellie.

When Mikhail slept, holding her later that night, Ellie knew she had to protect him and his family. Just as he'd protected her and hers….

"You miss Ellie already, eh? And she's only taking a weekend away." Fadey reached to turn off his saw and then the vibrant accordion music he liked while working in the shop. He ran a loving hand over the walnut cabinet that Mikhail was building and bent to critically inspect the drawers. "She will like that and the new sewing machine you got—so many gadgets and far more difficult than your mother's old machine. But I think you should give her that one instead. She has nothing of her mother. Such a sad story.... Use the new hardware for the drawers. It is more suitable. More like a woman.''

"She's gone to see Paul.'' Mikhail removed the red bandanna he had been wearing across his forehead and brushed the sawdust from his face with it. He tested the wooden dowels into the holes he had drilled and fought the memory of the bitter argument he'd had with Ellie as she'd packed to drive to Seattle.

In the end, they'd settled for an uneasy compromise. Because her car was fine for short distances, but wasn't in top repair, she would drive his BMW.

"He is her father. That little one is torn apart by love, and by you, too. Have patience. Do not be so angry—she is not JoAnna. Trust her.''

Mikhail threw down the wooden dowel he had been measuring. He wanted to go after Ellie, to protect her, because Paul didn't have his daughter's ability to love. And because the memory of Hillary striking Ellie was too fresh.

With a tender smile, Fadey opened the plastic container Mary Jo had sent. He lifted it to inhale the clove and cinnamon scent as though it were heaven. "Here, have some of your mother's cookies. No one makes them like her. They are like little kisses, eh? From your mother?''

Mikhail looked at the clock and knew that by this time, Ellie was in her father's mansion, battling for Tanya and for him.

"I don't like her doing my fighting for me.''

Fadey offered the cookies to him, and Mikhail ate one without tasting. Fadey's big hand rested on his son's shoulder, shaking him gently, affectionately, in the way of a compassionate father and a man who also missed his love. "She came to you because she needed help. Now, she looks at you with love and sometimes with sadness. Women are different, Mikhail. She has raised her sister and still loves her, in spite of her selfishness. Ellie remembers Hillary as a baby, as a little girl, and so those memories tangle around her, even as she fights her sister. But she loves Tanya like a mother would a child, and she is emotionally torn between everyone, including you. Let her do what she must. You cannot interfere or protect her this time. She has strengths, that Ellie, or she could not have kept Tanya safe this long.''

''Ellie hasn't called.'' Mikhail needed to hear the sound of her voice, to know that she was safe. He rubbed the ache in his chest, the loneliness without her.

''She wants this ended. She wants her daughter to come to a safe home with no problems.''

''A man like Paul knows how to wait for just the right moment.''

''So she is a woman, trying to protect her nest and her loves. Understand that. She'll come back to you,'' Fadey said as he gave Mikhail a big hug and kissed his cheek. ''She'll come back to you, and meanwhile you are making something nice for her. It is hard to wait, but she is doing what she must—just as you are doing what you must.''

She'd only been gone two nights—staying Friday night in her father's mansion and then Saturday in a hotel, putting herself back together.

Yet as Ellie carried her bag up the steps to the small cabin on Sunday evening, she felt as if a lifetime had passed. Tired and worn and aching, she had to come back to the cabin instead of the Amoteh. Of all the places that she had lived, this alone was home.

She couldn't face Mikhail just yet. Facing Paul, tit for tat, the bitterness running between them, she didn't like herself. An aging playboy, Paul didn't like the reality of how empty his life was, despite the women and the parties.

Most of all, he feared the loneliness of old age and no one really caring for him.

Ellie knew that, and in the heat of an argument, she'd

used it. "You can pay all the girlfriends, and nurses and companions you want, but you're going to end up alone."

In that instant, she saw the first fear in Paul's face and regretted her thrust at him.

The battle with her father raged in her mind, his accusations, her brittle defenses gathered from years of fighting and surviving. He'd said that Hillary had no one to organize her upcoming birthday party and she needed to make an impression on her Wall Street fiancé... Tanya was young; she would forget Ellie as her mother, and the girl would have everything—

Hillary. Ellie's little sister, now grown and on a path of self-destruction, taking others with her—that wouldn't be Tanya, Ellie promised.

She stepped inside the cabin's shadows and closed the door behind her, dropping her bag. She leaned against the door and closed her eyes, letting the dark warmth and safety enfold her.

Tanya could have everything that Hillary and she had had, but love and patience wouldn't be in the mix.

Mikhail was going to lose everything—

She touched the new cabinet beneath the window overlooking the beach. All the Stepanov furniture in the cabin was heavily built, but this cabinet seemed like a small desk. Obviously new, the walnut wood carried the scent of the Stepanovs' furniture polish and drawers ran down the sides, the hardware pulls more feminine that the usual heavy metal designs.

The shadows stirred and the overhead light blinded her. "Mikhail?"

"It's for you," he said coming toward her. "The new sewing machine is on the floor, and my mother's old one is in the cabinet. You can have your choice. Leigh said that sewing relaxes you. I thought you might need that now."

In a dark red sweater and jeans and a heavy growth of stubble on his jaw, his hair mussed, the waves standing out in odd peaks, Mikhail had never been more appealing.

Aware that he was studying her, Ellie tried to smooth the tendrils that had escaped her ponytail. Her dark sweat-suit looked as though she had slept in it, which she had—if she'd slept at all. She fought tears as Mikhail drew her against him. "I don't want to talk about it."

"You don't need to."

Ellie struggled back from his arms. "Because of me, you might lose everything. Paul wasn't in a listening mood, and I wasn't sweet. I'm his daughter, after all."

Mikhail framed her face with his hands. "You're the woman I love. And you have said that you love me. Isn't that enough?"

She slashed away the tears on her cheek. "This is an uncommon situation, Mikhail. Your resort, your life's work and ambition and Tanya's welfare—"

His head went back as though she'd slapped him, those green eyes flashing. "I will provide for you. Trust me."

Ellie took a deep breath and served him news she knew he wouldn't like. "I made a deal with Paul. He wants the Lathrops to look like a family—appearances matter, you know, the perfect picture…and Mikhail, I do love my sister. These things are so important to her."

"And you are important to me." Mikhail's open hand hit the table, and the salt shaker and peppermill rattled. "Paul couldn't wait. He called the instant you left. You agreed to arrange Hillary's birthday party, and the engagement one, too. I told him you might reconsider once we've talked. The question is, where have you been since you left him on Saturday afternoon?"

"I tried to talk with Hillary—"

Mikhail's hand shot out to capture her face, turning it for his inspection. "Did she hit you?"

"No.… She's my little sister," Ellie heard herself cry, echoes of the bitter argument cutting her like icy sleet.

"And you love her. You love everyone, don't you? And it's tearing you apart," he murmured, his deep voice soft and curling around her. "You've been a mother to them both, a selfish father and a sister needing you, and most of all, you've given an unloved child your heart. And you want to protect me. Are you going to let me hold you now?''

"Don't you see, Mikhail? Paul is going to ruin everything—''

He shrugged and smoothed her hair back from her cheek, his thumbs brushing the earrings he had given her. ''I don't think so. Where did you stay last night?''

"At a hotel. I just couldn't face—'' Mikhail picked her up and sat, holding her in a big rocker.

"If anything had happened to you, my life would have been so empty,'' he said unevenly against her temple. ''I ask that you do not tear yourself apart even more, that you allow Hillary to chose her own path and only help her when it doesn't hurt you so. I ask that you do not act as Paul's hostess.''

"I had to give him something to make a tentative truce. He can be horrible, Mikhail—you know him.''

"Do you not know me?'' he asked gently.

"What can you do?''

"Love you. Hold you. Organize all the managers of Mignon International in a walkout.''

She sat up, staring at him. ''You can't do that.''

His eyebrow lifted in a challenge. ''Can I not?''

Ellie eased to her feet, terrified that the nightmare had grown to touch others' lives. ''Mikhail, you wouldn't. Those people have worked so hard to build their own careers. So have you.''

He nodded and watched her pace the length of the cabin. ''Top people who can get top jobs instantly with a brand-new rising company, already in place and searching for managers. The offers for me to take over other chains have been coming in since the Amoteh's success. I can run a competing chain from right here. I have old friends who will back me, too. And there is damage I can do before leaving Mignon. I know the infrastructure better than Paul. It would all be legal, of course. He knows that.''

Mikhail stood and placed his hands in his jeans pockets. ''The main problem now is if you like the sewing machine. If you don't want Mom's old one, then the new machine can be easily fitted into the cabinet. I needed something to do while you were gone—otherwise I would have come after you. I had already started it, but—''

''He's jealous of you.'' Ellie's outburst surprised her, an understanding that came on that heartbeat.

''Yes.''

''Why?''

Mikhail slowly ran his hand over the smooth wood of the sewing cabinet. ''Because he senses that he doesn't have you anymore. He is afraid.''

''He told you that?''

''No, but I know how I would feel, if another man took you away from me.''

Ellie scrubbed her face as she tried to fit all the pieces into a sane picture; it seemed that Mikhail had compassion for a man who had none, for a man who threatened to take everything from him. ''Bliss sent him love beads and Ed sent him a worry stone. They were on his desk. He was actually rubbing that worry stone.''

''That's what they do—Leigh's parents love. So do you.'' He frowned slightly and added, ''Are you going to make me wait for you? Tell me what you think of this cabinet, mmm?''

Mikhail studied his work and lifted a chair to place it in front of the cabinet. ''Is it too tall? Here, sit in this chair. I can shorten the cabinet's legs or make a chair that suits you—yes, that is what I'll do, make a chair for you.''

As if just remembering, he turned suddenly and lifted the portable sewing machine from the floor and placed it on the cabin's table, opening the case. The deluxe sewing machine, complete with electronic buttons and gadgets she'd probably never use, seemed to fascinate Mikhail. Ellie struggled to move from the trauma of the past two days, the emotional homecoming to Mikhail, to his admiration of the new sewing machine. He leaped over major problems to the simplest one—did she like the gift he made for her? "I—it's beautiful."

"It is truly beautiful wood," he stated critically, a man who had helped his father build the furniture company and who enjoyed textures. He ran his hand over the gleaming wood, caressing it. "It's walnut. I thought of cherry, but walnut was at hand and I needed to work with my hands as I thought of you. But what do you think of the cabinet?" he asked sternly, his arms crossed.

Ellie sat very carefully in front of the sewing machine. There was a formality about Mikhail that she recognized as boyish eagerness, disguised as only a man would. She smoothed the wood with both hands, adoring the gift, and the man. "I love it. No one has ever made anything for me before—except for Tanya's drawings and her macaroni necklaces."

"Those are important gifts." He moved quickly, opening the lid to flatten into a shelf beside the machine. "Here. That is my mother's old machine, and it does a few things…good for denim, she says. When Jarek and I were young, she was always patching…there wasn't that much money. She likes her new machine better…it's like the one on the table, but not good for the heavier weight. I can change them easily, whichever you prefer—or…"

"Your mother's old machine?"

"Jarek, Dad and I talked. You have nothing of *your* mother's, and it might appeal to you more to have something of *my* mother's. Foolish, yes, but we meant well." Mikhail's deep voice had that lick of accent that said he was deeply emotional. "You should have something of a mother, Ellie, something handed down to you. If not this, then something else."

She could have cried then, shattering so easily. But then

Mikhail would have worried. "Thank you," she managed humbly.

Mikhail grinned and lifted the machine head to stand upright. "See?"

Ellie couldn't breathe, her emotions swirling around her. In another minute, she would turn into sobbing mess. Deep within her, she'd always ached for the mother that was never there, for some small part to remember.... "It's lovely."

Mikhail kneeled to open and close the drawers on either side of the leg space. He lifted out a small basket, filled with sewing goods. "Mom said that she and Tanya went shopping and are sending you all the things you'll need. Meanwhile, Leigh brought a few things—some material, scraps that she said you'd need to play with, her sewing scissors, some thread."

He looked longingly back at the super model on the table. "I can change them easily. It was only a thought to put Mother's in the cabinet, instead of the new one. Which one do you like?"

"The one and only—you," she whispered as she framed his face with her hands and bent to kiss him. Mikhail's arms circled her legs.

"Did you miss me?" he asked rawly between her tiny, hungry kisses.

"Only this much," Ellie said as she fused her lips to his.

Mikhail awoke to the smooth whir of the sewing machine and turned slowly on his side to watch Ellie sewing by candlelight. By her random actions, the testing of the tension and thread, he knew she was testing the machine and making it hers—

Lying in the shadows, he knew she was struggling against her fear for the Amoteh and his family, and her love of her father and sister.

Then she turned as if sensing him, attuned to his heartbeat as he was to hers. Ellie blew the candle out and rose, taking off his T-shirt as she walked toward him. In the dim light the earrings he had given her swayed and gleamed.

Mikhail held his breath as the moonlight outlined her body, the dip and curve of waist to hip, the rounded shadow of her breasts, the darkening between her thighs. Hidden by shadows, her face was framed by the tousled lengths of her hair.

She slid into his arms as if she were coming home, and moved over him, watching him as they slowly became one, the smooth friction between their bodies already flowing and heating.

Moving smoothly over him, holding him intimately, tightly, Ellie's eyes locked with his as if she wanted to remember him like this forever....

He knew her body too well, and it was telling him a secret her lips kept from him.

Mikhail turned her quickly, rising above her. He held her hands beside her head, watched the heat pulse beneath that smooth skin, watched her eyes half close as she went inside herself and the constrictions held him tightly.

"I'm not the woman for you," she whispered unevenly, and he knew that was what she'd kept from him—her fear.

"Are you not?" he challenged, deliberately holding her on that delicate peak, his passion mixed with frustration.

"This isn't fair," she whispered, crying out as Mikhail began to move again, filling her.

"I'm a fair man, but not in this. Tell me again that we are not meant for each other...tell me now," he demanded, even as he held his body in check, needing more from her than the physical mating to make him complete.

She fought him silently, her eyes lashing at him. "Okay, I love you," she said finally when he lifted his mouth from her breasts, licking them into peaks.

Even now, she was fighting him. He admired her pride, but he could have nothing less than the truth between them. "And?"

She squirmed restlessly beneath him, and his blood

pulsed hot and wild with the need to take her. But he wouldn't, not just yet.

"And you're not nice, Mikhail. You wear a suit and you can look like ice, but I know you for what you are. You take what you want and you're not sweet."

He moved against her and watched her go into herself just that heartbeat, her legs tightening to hold him. He needed that, to be held and tormented by her, just as he was demanding the truth from her. "And are you not taking what you want?"

"You know that I am."

He nuzzled her cheek and moved deeper into the lock of her body, rocking gently. "I am only a man who has missed you."

"You're deliberately tormenting me," Ellie whispered between her teeth as she caught his hair in her fist and brought his lips down to hers. The savagery of the gesture was what he wanted—truth. "Now finish the job."

The emotions that had been simmering in him erupted. "I always finish what I start. Next time, don't spend the night cowering in a hotel. You come back to me. We are one, together. Just as I share your body and you share mine, we share our lives, our fears and pain. Do not ever hold yourself from me. I never want to feel so helpless again."

"Helpless? You?"

"Never stay away from me again," he repeated unevenly.

"I didn't want you to see me in pieces."

"I have seen you in pieces before—lovely, soft, melting, pieces. That I was happy to accomplish with your assistance. I believe we could handle your problems in much the same manner—give and take. You are my woman, Ellie. It may be old-fashioned, but that's what you are. You belong to me. I belong to you."

She stared up at him. "Arrogant, primitive, macho—"

"You can get a little primitive yourself. I could use that for reassurance," he said fiercely.

"Just let me at you," she returned as fiercely, her fingers laced with his own. "You're setting terms for our relationship at the wrong time, bud…ah—"

Her body arched as Mikhail moved to prove his point.

She pushed at him, thrashing her head upon the pillow, and Mikhail couldn't help laughing as he drew her back.

"You're playing with me—you great big—"

"But I love to play with you. You can play with me," he invited quite reasonably and waited for her next move.

Ellie began to laugh, that rich full laugh that said he had her complete attention, that the tension and sadness that had wrapped around her earlier were completely gone. Then they began to move together, watching each other, completing each other.…

The wild storm surged upon them, her nails digging into his back, breaking his control, her lips hungry and open and demanding, her taste filling his mouth as they flew over the edge of the world and out into the stars.…

He took her once more before dawn, gently this time, listening to those sweet, sleepy sounds as she gave herself to him. When she curled against him, her arm around him, her head on his shoulder, Mikhail lay quietly, listening to her breathe.

He gathered her closer and knew that he would do anything to keep her.…

Would she hate him for what he had done?

Nine

Ellie hurried down the hallway to Mikhail's office. At ten o'clock, she'd slept deeply, awakening to an empty bed and her body well-loved and completely drained and relaxed. She hummed through a hurried shower and shampoo, a stop at her suite to change into a navy blue sweater and slacks, and hoped she could just put her body in one place with her mind.

Her body wanted to cuddle to Mikhail, and enjoy the after play of good, satisfying lovemaking with just that touch of tenderness, that pause and nuzzle and sigh that told her of his pleasure.

Her mind wanted to make him pay for setting terms so fiercely last night, when she had no basic defense, only her hunger for the man she loved—for the man who loved her.

On the other hand, she wasn't on edge anymore, she was completely rested and ready to present the résumé of the female golf pro to Mikhail. Drue Gannon had had enough of competition and traveling on the professional circuit, and she wouldn't fold when the pressure got rough; she also knew that in working for a resort, there was more to her job than teaching. Quiet, determined, Drue knew how to focus on the realities and compromises that went with dealing with the public.

Ellie nodded to Edna as she flew by, anxious to get Mikhail to agree to putting Drue on Amoteh's payroll.

"Ellie, wait—Mikhail said you were taking the day off." Edna's voice was a little higher than usual, but Ellie rushed on, happy and eager to see Mikhail.

"Catch you later, Edna." She smiled, anticipating seeing Mikhail, and rapped briefly before entering his office.

The spacious masculine office vibrated with tension, an ominous silence shrouding the room.

Her father sat in the chair opposite Mikhail's desk, and Paul's dark red face said he was angry. Mikhail's expression was impassive, and unlike last night, he was perfectly groomed—only a lover would notice the dark love-bite on his throat, just above his pristine white collar.

Ellie instantly recognized Mikhail's anger. Only a lover could see beyond his cool expression to that narrowed gleam between his lashes and the taut ridge of muscle crossing his cheek and jaw.

The men's tension ricocheted silently around the room, pricking at her. She knew that one man could be as tough as the other, and yet, dressed for business, the men were alike on the surface, and so different in their values.

On Mikhail's desk stood a sewing serger, a machine used to finish seams and hems in fine material and to embroider. An assortment of threads used by it lay tangled and discarded. Tall spools of thread gleamed nearby. In the center of his desk was an open file of large glossy black and white photographs. Shadows seemed to ripple across them like clouds brewing a storm.

"Good morning, Ellie," Mikhail said smoothly as an array of Tanya's crayon drawings danced on the wall behind him. Only the slight tensing of his jaw gave any indication that he was angry. "Paul and I were just discussing the man you've been seeing. Apparently Lars took pictures of you and this man and sent them to Paul."

Mikhail snapped the file closed. "Sit down, Ellie. Since you're here, I want you to see these. What you tell Paul is your decision."

Paul was on his feet, rocking on his heels, his hands behind him as he stared out of the window at the small town of Amoteh. "She's been playing you for a fool, Mikhail. She's set you up to defend her and Tanya, and then she's playing around with another man."

Paul's opinion of his daughter didn't matter; she'd known since childhood that he'd never gotten over his wayward mother and held that against all women, even his daughters. Ellie's hand shook as she eased into a chair and slowly opened the file Mikhail had handed her. "Lars took these?"

"Apparently, when Hillary's kidnapping idea failed, Lars had a better idea—spying for Paul—before he decided to take a trip away from Amoteh."

"For the record, I didn't approve of Hillary being so roughshod with my granddaughter," Paul stated harshly.

Kaleidoscope images of Tanya as a baby left untended and later as a girl terrified at the day care center when Hillary decided to take her by force, ran through Ellie's mind. "You're a little late with that, Paul."

Paul swore darkly. "You're not keeping me from her. Hillary says you're lying about how she treated Tanya."

"Maybe you should have taken the time to see for yourself, Paul. But then you have two daughters *you* ignored as children, don't you?"

"Get over it," Paul said fiercely. "You got what you needed."

"Did I? Let's just say that I know what Tanya needs." The photographs were of Ellie looking up at a big man, dressed in a worn sweatshirt and jeans, his face unseen, as he braced his hands beside her head on the weathered boards of the pier, as he lay over her on the beach, as he carried her over his shoulder. She laughed up at him, the wind blowing her hair as she smoothed his; another picture was that of her hands framing his face, her eyes closed as she kissed him. The sensual, intimate views of her face always obscured the man's.

That man was Mikhail. Lars was playing games with blackmail. No doubt he intended to also approach Mikhail with a second set of pictures that revealed his identity if Mikhail didn't comply with his conditions.

Mikhail had given her the choice to tell Paul of their relationship, their love, or to deny it.

"I think," she said slowly, as she attempted to align her hurried morning with the clash between her father and her lover, two strong men, "that perhaps a cup of tea would be in order. I'll be right back."

Paul snickered. "I raised Ellie and Hillary. They're like their mothers...unfaithful."

"Perhaps they needed a faithful man, one who recognized his marriage vows," Mikhail said quietly.

Paul turned immediately, leaning forward in a fighting posture, his fists at his side. "You don't know anything."

Mikhail leveled a cool look at Ellie. "Now would be a good time to get the water for the *samovar.*"

"I'm not leaving. You are not dismissing me." *Mikhail had wanted his conversation with her father to be very private; he'd deliberately exhausted her so that she would oversleep and miss Paul.*

"You are excused," Mikhail said firmly, spacing his words.

He'd been so thorough in making love to her, and now he treated her like the employee she was.

"Did you know that Paul would be here in this morning?" she asked more lightly than she felt as her happiness shattered into shards at her feet.

Mikhail's grim expression didn't falter. "Yes. We had

an appointment for Monday morning at eleven. He was a bit early.''

''I see. And I was a bit late.''

''No doubt you were tired from your trip,'' he said too coolly. ''It's understandable. You may leave now.''

She wasn't just his employee—she was his lover. And she loved him. He would not wage her wars but banish her from the battle scene. ''No.''

Mikhail's jaw tightened. ''What Paul and I have to say is private.''

Ellie stood and gripped the file she had been holding, then she slapped it onto the desk. Her eyes locked with Mikhail's as she said, ''Let's get this all out in the open, since dear old Lars has been spying on me—no doubt for a good price. The man in those pictures is Mikhail.''

She frowned slightly as a new idea hit her. Danya and Alexi's visit had also been planned. ''Did Lars just accidentally decide to take a trip when your cousins dropped in for that short visit?''

''He seemed to think it was a good idea,'' Mikhail said coolly.

Paul looked as if he would explode. ''You want my daughter to get your hands on Mignon, a company I built. Well, it won't work, Stepanov. I'll cut her off.''

Mikhail took his time in answering the accusation, and his eyes never left Ellie's. ''She has been managing without your money for some time. I want Ellie because I love her. I want to marry her, Paul. I want Tanya to be my daughter. And you've done enough damage to Ellie. She's tried to hold a family together that didn't matter to you. Now, don't you think it's time you told her about her mother?''

''That woman? No. And don't think you hold all the cards here, Stepanov. I'll break you.''

Mikhail's quiet answer was brisk, and this time he turned to look at Paul. ''I think not. Whether Ellie decides to marry me or not, you will not interfere with the Amoteh, or with her as Tanya's mother. If you do, I will make it my life's pleasure to ruin you.''

The men were battling on without Ellie, threatening each other while she was awash with confusion.

''What about my mother?'' Ellie remembered Nora's voice pleading with her over the telephone. The infrequent calls had begun when she was thirty, but Ellie wouldn't speak to the woman who had deserted her. With Tanya as her daughter, Ellie's resentment toward Nora had deepened. No loving mother could have left her child....

''I'm getting out of here,'' Paul said roughly as he brushed by Ellie.

''Take this. Your granddaughter drew it. She's a wonderful, loving child. Ellie has done a good job as a parent, and you're not harming her as you did your daughters.'' Mikhail stood and removed one of Tanya's drawings taped to his wall. He handed it to Paul, who crushed it in his fist as he shoved out the office door, slamming it behind him.

''What about Nora?'' Ellie turned to Mikhail, who had that guarded expression.

''I wanted Paul to tell you, but he can't admit his own wrongdoing. I contacted your mother. As hard as you have fought for Tanya, I couldn't see her leaving you with Paul. If you want to know the whole story, not the one Paul fed you as you grew up, call her.'' Mikhail handed Ellie a paper with a telephone number written in his bold handwriting.

''You had no business interfering in that. *Not that.*'' A nightmare of memories swirled around her, the child deserted by an unloving mother and ignored by a harsh, cold, demanding father. The ten-year-old who promised that her baby sister would have all her love.

''Did I not?'' he asked too quietly, reminding her of last night, when he'd held her, demanding her admission of love and that they were of one body and one heart.

But Ellie was too shaken by the encounter with Paul and by Mikhail contacting a woman she never wanted to see.

"You deliberately exhausted me last night to waylay me from meeting Paul."

"I was under the impression that it was to our mutual agreement and satisfaction. Take the rest of the day off. I don't want the Amoteh destroyed by your mood, and the way you look now, you're going to war. And by the way, I do love you and want to marry you."

With that, Mikhail sat down to place spools of thread on the serger, studying the directions and clearly dismissing her. In his big hands, the gleaming threads looked as fragile as Ellie felt.

"You'll never figure that out," she stated, and in a fury hurried to quickly maneuver all the threads into the machine.

Mikhail scowled at the machine and then at her. She had the distinct impression that she had taken away his toy as he spoke. "If you decide to keep it, I thought the new sewing machine might be well placed in your suite. This one is not for plain sewing, rather for finish work. It makes scalloped edges and—"

"I know what it does. I've wanted one my whole life. I'm getting that golf pro, Stepanov. Here's Drue's résumé…and don't ever arrange my life again. And the next time you decide to have a lovemaking marathon to get me out of the action, I'll be prepared."

He lifted that mocking eyebrow. "Oh, really?"

While she struggled for words, Mikhail nodded. "Listen to your mother, Ellie. Nora is a good woman. She didn't desert you. It wasn't that simple. Other lives were involved. She did what she had to do, and the choices weren't easy. Now take some time to deal with this," he added before turning to reading the day's mail, making a show of ignoring her.

Ellie looked at that dark hair gleaming in the sunlight and did what she had to do. She picked up the golf pro's file and slapped him over the head. Mikhail tensed, then he continued reading. "Call her. The marriage offer stands."

She couldn't pick through the storm of her emotions—confusion, the sense of being betrayed, her need to have him hold her tight. Her instincts, fostered by years of family infighting, said to protect herself. Yet Mikhail had just gambled everything he'd built for her; she could ruin him and many other lives. In the end, he could hate her. "And if I refuse?"

Mikhail's eyes flickered just slightly, that muscle tensed in his jaw, but he spoke coolly. "Then we continue to work as we have before. You're a valuable asset to the Amoteh. Your skills would be difficult to replace."

She stared at him, unable to merge this cold man into the lover who had held her so tenderly last night. Words churned and boiled furiously in her mind. They wouldn't come to her lips. In the end, she settled for action—tossing all the neat stacks of paper on his desk into the air. As they fluttered through the air, she batted them, then methodically circled the room. She briskly tilted all the pictures on the wall, and pushed the chairs into different positions.

On an afterthought, she rearranged his desk, placing the intercom on his left side, instead of his right, his appointment calendar centered next to him, the small gold clock in the middle of the desk.

As she walked by him, Mikhail held out the file of pictures.

"Thanks," she said briskly and left with as much dignity as she could manage before she started crying.

Mikhail regretted his last words to Ellie. Once again, he'd used his business shields to conceal the passion of his heart. He ached for her. His discussion with Paul was meant to protect her from the harshest realities of her family. And then, suddenly, when she arrived, the meeting began spinning out of control, and he'd served the offer of marriage to her as he would a contract. Ellie's pale face had tortured him since that morning.

However, she had apparently recovered. Mikhail

frowned as he watched the tall, handsome man lean close to her on the golf course. The visiting film star's body language said he was definitely interested in Ellie, and her bright smile said she wasn't exactly refusing what he offered. The wind blew her hair around her head, and her companion gently smoothed it back.

Mikhail tensed; he knew what her hair felt like, rich and silky in his hands, dragging along his bare skin.

The movie star liked preparation, and was checking out the Amoteh's golf course before entering the tournament there in June. Russell Ward had everything a woman could want, including charm. His arm around Ellie's shoulders wasn't rebuffed and her head lifted with a burst of laughter. They stopped again at the door to the Amoteh's indoor pool, talking intimately, and Russell smiled as he flicked the earring she wore.

Mikhail's gift to her.

At least she was still wearing them, even if she was furious with him.

Mikhail rammed his hand through his hair. He'd wanted to protect her....

Russell bent to kiss her cheek, and Mikhail found himself moving toward them. If the door had been locked, he might have torn it from its hinges. "Russell, I hope you're enjoying the Amoteh."

"I truly am. I like to check out the layout before entering any celeb tournament. I usually plan my moves." Russell's gaze was warm and appreciative as he looked at Ellie. "Where's the best place to eat around here?"

"Our restaurant is very good."

Russell's smile at Ellie was intimate. "Something more private?"

Ellie's stare at Mikhail revealed nothing, and he could have grabbed her and carried her away. Just that lift of her chin, that slash of her eyes, told him that she was furious with him. "You can always order up to your room," she offered.

Russell's devastating and cosmetically perfect smile widened. "I'll do that."

"Yes, do," Mikhail said too sharply, and decided he had better remove himself from the temptation of smashing Russell's expensive teeth.

Hours later, Jarek eased down into the chair next to Mikhail's at the Seagull's Perch. "You look like you've had a hard day. It's been a long time since you've brooded in a corner like this, looking as if you could kill someone."

"Lay off. I just asked Ellie to marry me, and she's at the hotel with Russell Ward, having a nice 'intimate' dinner."

"Okay. So why is she headed this way and looking as if she could wring your neck?"

Mikhail looked up just in time to be hit by a balled piece of paper. It bounced into his glass, floating in the beer.

"Hi, Jarek. You might not want to stay. Mikhail just pulled his big brother protector act with me and I'm not having it.... There's your note, Mikhail, telling me to take the day off," Ellie said flatly. She hitched up the straps to her tote bag to her shoulder. "I missed it on the table this morning, but then I slept late and was in a hurry to get to work."

She looked at Jarek and shifted the Amoteh tote bag she was carrying to her other hand. "By the way, Jarek, did you know that Danya and Alexi were hauled in to muscle Lars out of here?"

Jarek looked at Ellie and then at Mikhail. "Mmm. I had an idea. Lars isn't a friendly sort of guy to the Stepanovs, and Hillary had paid him a lot of money. He needed a vacation from Amoteh."

"I see. A conveniently arranged vacation. Mikhail likes to arrange things, doesn't he? Where exactly is Lars taking this vacation?"

"Um... I think he's learning how to be a cowboy somewhere in Wyoming. Well, it's been nice. I'd better get home."

Neither Mikhail nor Ellie replied or watched Jarek leave. "So how is Russell?" Mikhail said finally.

"Gorgeous. Charming. We got along fine. He's entering the tournament, encouraging his buddies to come. We'll be packed with celebrities and the PR opportunities will be more than we hoped. I'm arranging a special party for Russell in his suite. We need that golf pro on site to help us. Did you check out Drue's résumé?"

"And are there going to be more than two at this special party? Or just you and Russell?"

Elle's eyes narrowed at him. Rita came to ask if Ellie wanted a drink; she stopped when she noted Mikhail's scowl and Ellie's frown. The waitress turned and walked back to the bar.

Ellie put her hands on the table and scanned the various men who were watching with interest. She looked back at Mikhail. "This place is a cave where men hang out to avoid what's coming to them. Do you want this public, or private?"

Mikhail felt very fragile. Ellie's eyes said she had been crying, and now she was mad. He wasn't certain if he should try to comfort her—if she would let him—or let her just have at him. To be uncomfortable with his actions, to realize that he could be a jealous man, and one uncertain of his beloved's next move caused Mikhail to be wary. One wrong move and she'd... "Are you going to throw things?"

"I might. But then, you're a big strong hero. You can fix it, can't you? Just like you want to fix everything in my life."

On their way to the cabin, Ellie walked ahead of Mikhail, her hips swaying, and he tried not to think of making love to her.

The forbidding look over her shoulder said this might not be a good time.

"Do you think I like being compared to your ex-wife?" Ellie asked as she pivoted to face Mikhail, her body taut.

She tossed the tote bag filled with material and thread onto the table. "The package from your mother came today. She has lovely taste in fabric and patterns."

He closed the door slowly, the merry tinkling of the wind chimes in contrast to the storm brewing within the cabin. "There is no comparison between my ex-wife and you."

"She played you, didn't she? Used you? Tried to make you jealous with other men? I saw that today, when you...bristled at Russell. JoAnna certainly did a neat knife job on you. You can't trust me. *You can't trust me to make my own decisions.* I've handled men like him all my life—especially those who wanted Paul's money through me. I'm not a business. I'm a woman who has been on her own for a long time. Don't try to fix my life, Mikhail. It's too late. Don't you ever try to pull something like you did with Paul today. I've fought him all my life and—"

"And you're not alone anymore, Ellie. I wanted to help."

Pain went careening through her. "I love you. I trusted you and you hurt me."

"I am sorry."

He'd tried to help and had just opened up the painful past that she had worked so hard to forget. "Don't you invite Nora here. If you do, I'll leave, no matter what the situation. I'll go to Texas and get Tanya and—"

"Ellie..."

His soft tone sliced through her fear. She'd protected herself for years and now Mikhail wanted to bridge the years-old distance of a mother and daughter. "I can't call Nora, Mikhail. You don't understand. My family isn't like yours."

"She isn't the woman you think, Ellie, and she's paid a high price to protect her family, just as you have."

Ellie brushed the tears from her face. "What do you mean?"

"Talk with her first. Listen. And then make up your mind."

She felt herself spinning, old pain mixed with new fears. "I'm coming apart, Mikhail. First you and Paul, and then—"

"I meant well. I love you and I know how frightened you are."

Frightened? She was terrified. "And you want to marry me. You want to marry me, wasn't that what you said? I've lived with what Paul wanted—not asked, mind you, but wanted—most of my life. I was right. You are alike."

"That was a mistake," Mikhail admitted slowly. "My plans were different. I meant to ask you at the right moment, but with the same end result."

He looked out of the window. "Do you really think that I want you because of the Lathrop fortune, or to engineer a takeover of your father's holdings?"

"Of course not...but you'll end up hating me, Mikhail. And I don't think I could bear that."

When Mikhail studied her, he smiled tenderly, sadly. "Do you have so little trust in me, that I do not know my own heart? That I do not recognize how you make me feel as if I can't wait for each heartbeat, for the excitement and comfort you bring me?"

How could he humble himself so much, lay himself open to pain? she thought, loving him, as he gently took her into his arms. "Trust me, Ellie," he whispered unevenly. "Just trust me."

He was asking her to face her past, to open up all the old pain and bitterness of a child left behind by an unloving mother. "I'm an emotional mess. I'm going to cry—and I *never* cry."

His hand stroked her hair, easing her head to his shoulder. "Maybe it's time you did."

Her closed hand beat lightly on his chest, her emotions tangled with his tenderness and what he was asking of her.

"I suppose you've already gotten the plane tickets for my visit with Nora."

"*Our* visit. We leave tomorrow. Jarek can handle any problems that might come up here in the next three days."

"You sure know how to whisk a girl off her feet, bud," Ellie whispered unevenly.

"I thought you might want to do that before Tanya comes back, or before Paul decides to act. Are you angry with me?" he asked so rawly that she knew he feared her reaction.

"Yes, but just don't stop holding me."

"I never will," Mikhail said as he picked her up and sat in the big rocking chair, holding her.

"I'm a little old for this, Mikie," she whispered in a voice filled with tears.

"Shh. You give me comfort, just holding you. You're brave, Ellie. Not every woman would face what she fears most. You have and fought every step of the way."

"You've fought your own battles." She thought of how Mikhail must have felt, the child he wanted very much taken away.

He kissed her forehead. "Well, then, together, I guess we can face anything. Right?"

She didn't answer, awash with memories of a child, rejected by her mother. "I can't promise to be nice. It's not in my genes."

"Sometimes 'nice' just covers what should be uncovered."

In the rental car seat beside him, Ellie sat stiffly, her face expressionless and pale and shadowed just as it had been on the plane.

Mikhail had gambled on Ellie's father and now her mother, and he could lose Ellie forever.

On the windswept coast of Maine, the tiny picturesque town's shops boasted of fresh lobster, hauled by the boats on the wharf, and handcrafted knitted goods. As Mikhail pulled the car to a stop across from a weathered general store, an elderly woman rode by, her bicycle's basket filled with a grocery sack.

Ellie inhaled and seemed to freeze as an older woman came from the store, out onto the porch. She talked to a man with a cane as she poured potatoes from the cup of her apron into a straw basket. The wind caught her hair, more gray than blond, but there was no mistaking the clear-cut features, or the lift of her chin as she scanned the clear spring day, raising her hand to wave at passersby. She paused to straighten a tower of wooden lobster traps and then pulled open the old door and entered the building. The sign overhead read, Taggert General Store, 1909.

"Let's leave." Ellie's voice was hushed, fearful.

Mikhail understood. He'd moved too quickly, but then when a man wants all of a woman, unclouded by her past— or his, he could make mistakes. "Okay."

When he started the car, Ellie's hand slid over his. "No, wait. We've come this far."

"You've come this far," he corrected, aching for her, and praying he hadn't misjudged Nora.

"I...I want to meet her. I've thought so much about what I would tell her, what I think of her," Ellie stated quietly. "Don't you leave us alone, Mikhail Stepanov."

Inside the cluttered general store, Nora was working behind the old counter, using a large scoop to pour beans into a paper sack. She weighed it on huge ancient scale and smiled at the striking couple entering the store.

Her hand went over her heart, and for a moment, she stood still as Ellie stared at her, gray eyes mirroring gray eyes, the shape of her face. In the next minute, Nora rounded the corner, quickly removing the large apron from her blouse and loose slacks and tossing it onto a basket of apples. "Hugh," she said to the elderly man sweeping the board floors, "watch the store for a minute, will you?"

Ellie couldn't move, her hand tight within Mikhail's big one. *This was her mother....*

"Hello, Ellie," Nora said gently, love shining in her eyes. "Would you like to have a cup of tea upstairs in my apartment?"

When Ellie couldn't speak, the past's pain merging with the present, Mikhail said gently, "She's tired."

"She's beautiful," Nora whispered, and her hand raised slightly as if she wanted to stroke Ellie's hair.

Her mother had deserted her.... Ellie moved her head away from Nora's hand. She wanted to run and hide and never face the next few minutes. One look up at Mikhail told her that he worried, that he waited for her decision. "Let's just get this over with," she said briskly.

Nora frowned slightly but asked about the drive to the remote community. Mikhail answered for Ellie.

The stairs were old and worn, sagging and creaking as Ellie followed Nora. The tiny apartment overlooked the wharves, the boats bobbing on the waves.

Nora set a hot water kettle on the little stove. "I hope this is all right with you. I have a house, but—"

"This is fine, Nora," Mikhail said as Ellie stood stiffly in the center of the room, chilled despite her navy blue sweater and slacks.

Ellie's voice surprised her, a froth of anger pouring from her. "How could you leave your own child?"

Nora's hands stopped and fluttered over the tray she'd been preparing. She inhaled, straightened, and turned slowly. "I was forced to—"

"I don't believe that. You didn't want the responsibility of being a mother. Paul told me so."

"Paul lies." Nora's tone was bitter, her gray eyes flashing like steel.

"You should have come back for me—"

Mikhail's hand smoothed Ellie's rigid back, warming her. "Let her talk, Ellie."

Nora's head went up, as proud as Ellie's. "There's no easy way to do this, but I am so sorry."

"Sorry? Sorry? You abandoned me."

Nora's mouth, so like Ellie's, firmed, and she squared her body, as if bracing herself against the past. "I was born right here, in this little apartment. My parents struggled all their lives to preserve what Dad's parents had left him. Paul came into port one day and I loved him desperately. What Paul wants, he gets. We were married, and when you came along, he was tired of me, a small-town girl with values that didn't match his. I wasn't up to his social needs and he already had another woman more to his taste by the time you were born. I wouldn't think of leaving you, and fought for all I could, and then he began to threaten that he'd ruin my parents."

Her face shadowed as if she remembered the past with pain, plowing through it with quiet words that had been held too long. "Life just stacks up sometimes and you have to work through it. By that time, Dad had had a heart attack and Mom a stroke. I was all they had, and I was their caregiver and ran the store, too. They both needed money for medical bills and more procedures. There was no money to fight Paul, and he just kept pushing. In the end, he won, and I signed an agreement that I wouldn't contact you until you were an adult. I have a copy. In it, he assures that my parents' medical expenses will be taken care of. They never knew. It would have killed them to know I'd traded my daughter for a few more years of their lives."

She seemed to wilt then, slumping into a old rocking chair near the window, where she watched the day as though she'd passed many days thinking about the past. "Both my mother and my father died right here, in this apartment, overlooking the harbor. It tore my heart out, Ellie. Lives depended on me. First my parents and then my husband. I did the best I could do. Paul is a powerful man. I wasn't able to fight him."

Ellie clutched Mikhail's hand and he eased her into a worn overstuffed chair. "I don't believe you."

Nora slowly opened a drawer and slid an envelope into Mikhail's hand. "This is a copy. The original is in the safety deposit box. I'm really, really sorry, Ellie. I didn't know what else to do. My parents died about six years later.''

Ellie read the paper that Mikhail handed to her. ''You could have come back later, when your parents died.''

Nora shook her head. ''I had remarried while they were alive—a good man, and I needed someone. I was barely holding on. Tom struggled for years with the cancer that finally took his life. He was in and out of hospitals for years. We did have children, two sons. One had medical problems, too, and—''

''I want to leave,'' Ellie said quietly, fiercely, as an avalanche of emotions pressed down on her. She had half brothers... Paul had forced Nora to desert her.... This new knowledge was overwhelming—she tried to absorb it, fit it into a new vision of reality—and failed.

Nora stood, facing Ellie. ''I don't blame you. Just know that I never once stopped thinking of you, of loving you.''

''He said you were unfaithful.''

Nora shook her head. ''I wasn't. I loved him, even when I saw what he was. I couldn't believe that he would want to tear you from me. But Paul doesn't share love or kindness, and he's going to regret that one day. I pray for him.''

Ellie wanted to run into the shadows and hide from what she already suspected was true. She'd lost a lifetime with her mother, and the years stood too firmly between them. She clutched the paper in her hand, shaking with emotions. ''I'm leaving.''

''Try to forgive me, Ellie. Here...'' Nora removed a locket from her throat and when Ellie didn't move, she gave it to Mikhail. ''That's a picture of my parents, your grandparents and myself. I left it for you, but Paul sent it back.''

''Thank you, Nora,'' Mikhail said as Ellie flew down the stairs.

She was shaking in the rental car when Mikhail arrived, easing into the car. When he opened his arms, she slid into them, her body shaking. ''Do you believe her?''

Against her hair, his voice was deep. "Yes. But it is for you to decide."

"Take me home, Mikhail."

In their hotel room that night, Ellie didn't eat, sitting quietly and watching the Boston city traffic snake beneath the window. She moved as Mikhail asked, allowing him to dress her for bed, to hold her in the night. During the cross-country flight, she stared at the clouds, her body in the seat next to his, but her mind far away.

At Amoteh that evening, he parked beside the cabin; Ellie had said she preferred it. Jarek arrived with dinner, and glanced at Ellie as she watched the ocean's rolling waves. Mikhail shook his head and Jarek left silently.

"Do you want to talk?" Mikhail asked as he served dinner by candlelight.

Ellie pushed the food on her plate with her fork. "No."

She'd gone within herself, keeping her pain from him. All he could do was to wait.

He wondered briefly if Kamakani's curse still held, if he could lose her.

"I'd like to be alone," Ellie said finally. "Do you mind?"

Did he mind? His heart was tearing apart, aching for her. "I understand. Here, this is yours," he said as the locket and chain spilled onto the table, gleaming in the candlelight, a tiny tie between mother and daughter.

Her head bent as she spoke quietly. "You should know, Mikhail, that I don't want children other than Tanya. That should disqualify me as wife material. You're a man who should have a family."

Another woman hadn't wanted his children, and momentarily that pain ricocheted through Mikhail, then it swivelled into anger. "Stop playing the martyr. Have I asked you to do anything but marry me?"

Ellie's gray eyes shot thunderbolts at him. "I'm not a martyr, and you didn't ask."

He smiled briefly at her lick of temper, the first emotion she'd shown since meeting Nora. "Then you will have to ask me. Good night."

Outside the cabin, the sound of the waves slid against the night and Mikhail lifted his face to Strawberry Hill and Kamakani's curse.

Had he lost Ellie? Had he pushed too far?

Ten

"**G**oing somewhere?" Mikhail asked as he stepped out of the midnight shadows next to Ellie's car. His deep voice held an ominous purr, as if he had been waiting for her.

The prickle of awareness that always caught her when Mikhail was near edged up her nape. Ragged with emotions and lack of sleep, Ellie had given up trying to wait until morning. She had to confront her father, to see his reaction to Nora's claim. After four hours of pacing the cabin, she'd decided that nothing could keep her from Paul.

If Nora's claim were true, then Ellie had lost a lifetime with a mother she'd thought deserted her.... And she had to know....

Mikhail towered over her, looking tough and foreign, his hair tossed by the salty wind, his jaw dark with stubble. He'd changed into jeans and black T-shirt beneath his brown leather jacket, his work boots scuffed and wide apart as if nothing could move him. Mikhail's eyes gleamed as he looked down at her. Clouds slid by the moon, shifting shadows on his face, but not softening the harsh planes, the tight set of his lips, and the grooves beside them.

"How did you know that I'd be leaving tonight?"

His answer was too logical, too Mikhail. "You're impetuous and you're not one to wait."

She clenched her fist so hard that the car's keys bit into her palm. "I have to. You know I do. I have to see Paul. If Nora is right, then he's—"

"He's what he is—street tough, wrangling for power and money. Nora didn't fit his plans. Or don't you believe that?"

Ellie couldn't rest until she knew— "I just want to face him, Mikhail."

He smoothed her cheek with his fingertip. "You haven't rested. This could wait until you're—"

"Now, Mikhail. I have to know now. I'd rather be driving than awake and tossing in bed."

He nodded, scanning the ocean's black waves. "You could have called me."

"I've got to do this by myself."

His head went back, the tilt arrogant as he silently watched her. Then his hand shot out to capture her hair, lifting it away from her ear. "So you're wearing them, then. Do you think of me?"

He was so much a part of her, her body tuned to his, feeling the tension riveting him in the moonlight. "You know that I do."

His prowling finger slid down her cheek to her throat where the slender gold chain rested. He tapped the locket lightly. "You believe her?"

A ripple of pain shot through her; Paul was capable of separating a mother and child. "I don't want to. I'll know when I see his face."

"Then take this with you," Mikhail said roughly, and tugged her to him, his mouth hot and wild and promising—

He released her abruptly, and Ellie struggled for balance. Mikhail was frustrated, aching for her, and she—

She reached for his jacket with both hands and tugged. He didn't move, then as if he moved at his own choosing, he stepped closer. "What?"

"You're coming with me. I need you."

"Do you?" Again the arrogance, a man whose pride had been nicked and needed salving.

"I want you to protect him. I'm not certain of what I might do."

His head inclined slightly. "And you love him."

She stood on tiptoe to brush her lips across his. "And you. I love you. But I'm so afraid. You should have that family, Mikhail."

His expression softened and his lips returned her light kiss. "Can we not let the future take care of itself?"

The slight accent said Mikhail spoke his innermost feelings and she couldn't help but love him more. "What if I'm the same as Paul, Mikhail? What if I have within me the potential to do what he's done?"

He smiled and waggled her head as would a big brother, before opening the BMW's door and easing her into it. "You don't."

In Paul Lathrop's Seattle mansion, Mikhail leaned against the shadows of the office, his arms crossed as he watched Ellie battle with Paul. Magnificent in the predawn from the windows and the soft lamp lighting, and her anger, Ellie's color was high, her eyes flashing, her body taut in a black sweater and jeans. She stalked across the office, her hair a storm as she moved, the tips catching the soft light.

It wasn't in Mikhail's nature to stand by while the woman he loved battled herself, the past and her father. And yet, he knew that Ellie would resent his interference.

That she would want to face Paul alone had hurt Mikhail.

That she needed him to be with her had eased that slight injury.

That she had grabbed him in the car before they entered the mansion and had kissed him desperately had made him go a little light-headed. "Hold me and tell me that you love me," she'd demanded fiercely.

The impromptu make-out session in the front seat of his BMW left Mikhail's body hard and humming and Ellie flushed and breathless. She had patted his cheek. "Thanks. I needed that. I can always count on you."

He had groaned. "Yes. I am quite dependable. And I plan to finish what you just started."

She'd smoothed back his hair that her fingers had rumpled and studied him critically. "I like sex with you. Correction—I love sex with you. And I like that hungry sexy look you're giving me now, because most of all you make me feel like a woman. But I also like other things. You're a good friend, Mikhail. Thank you."

"Are you going to pat me on the head, like everybody else does?" he had asked warily.

"It's because you're sweet and you deserve pats and hugs."

He couldn't help inviting, "You are most welcome to apply them in regions other than the top of my head."

Despite her current mission, the drama of it, Ellie had laughed outright. It was delighted laughter, rich and full, and Mikhail wanted to hear more.

Watching her attack Paul now in the luxurious office, Mikhail smiled briefly. In effect, he was Ellie's over two-hundred pound, six-foot-three good-luck piece. The idea pleased him; he realized he was smirking.

He shrugged mentally. As Ellie's good-luck piece, he had a right to smirk happily, yet he stilled his expression. A street-savvy fighter, Paul was too sharp not to pick up nuances of weaknesses and to play them.

"Explain this." Ellie slammed the paper Nora had given her onto Paul's desk. He paled as he read it, tossing it onto his desk.

In his pajamas and robe, Paul looked old and tired, and behind him on the paneled walls was Tanya's framed drawing. He looked at Mikhail in the shadows. "I've thought about this. You'd be an asset as a son-in-law. You can have her.''

''She makes up her own mind.''

''Do something, Mikhail. She's out of control.''

''You're on your own,'' Mikhail answered coolly. Ellie had paid high prices for her father's actions, and now she was battling her love for him.

Paul sighed tiredly, the lines and shadows of his once handsome face deepening. He took an antacid tablet from the large bottle on his desk and popped it into his mouth. ''Do we have to do this now?''

''Why would you do such a thing? Why did you lie to me?'' Ellie demanded rawly, standing in front of his desk, her arms crossed.

Paul studied her and looked past her to Mikhail. ''You two are a pair, fighters and bulldogs, the both of you. She's got more flash though. You just make certain you make your point. I should have seen it earlier.''

Ellie's open hand hit the desk. ''I want to know why you would do such a thing.''

Paul seemed to shrink within his satin robe. ''I loved Nora. But I needed—she didn't fit what I thought I needed. I was going up in the business and she couldn't cope with what I expected of her. It wasn't the first mistake, or the last, I made. But I couldn't go back and undo it. There was no point.''

''Wasn't there?'' Ellie asked fiercely. ''What about me? Didn't I have the right to know the truth?''

He sighed tiredly and leaned back in his chair, closing his eyes. ''You look like her, and you were a part of her. I didn't want her to take you away from me.''

''You lied to me. You said she didn't want me. Do you know how that affected my life? What about Hillary? Is that what you did with her mother, too?''

''No. Hillary's mother knew I still loved Nora, and she really did not want her child. It was easy to buy her off— if only...'' Paul's eyes opened slowly as if weighted by years. "I was raised on the street, Ellie, dog eat dog. It was wrong, but I didn't change when it came to Nora. I found a woman who resembled her, and who was what I needed. In my way, I hoped Nora would go on and find someone better. But I couldn't let you go. I did what I had to do to keep you."

Ellie's voice vibrated quietly in the expensive furnishings. "You are not getting Tanya, and neither is Hillary. If you even think about coming close to Tanya, I will spread this story all over the papers and shed enough light on your deals to make you a business liability."

Paul was silent, staring at her, as if haunted by another woman. "Tanya looks like Nora, too—what an ironic coincidence."

Mikhail came to stand beside Ellie, watching her expressions war between love of her father and what he had done. Mikhail placed his hand on Ellie's back, felt the taut muscles there, the quivering anger in her body for all the years she'd missed with Nora. "Shall we go? It's enough for now?" he asked, anxious for her.

"It's not enough," she stated firmly, bitterly.

"For now," he pressed, aching for her. "You can't unravel the past within minutes."

"I just have."

She turned and walked out of Paul's office, not stopping until she was in the car. When Mikhail entered and revved the smooth engine, Ellie sat rigidly in the shadows. "He wants to give me to you to make a business deal. How typical."

As Mikhail drove, Ellie said, "I was proud of you. I really was. I expected you to charge in and try to fix everything. Then I would have had to handle the both of you."

"But you did that nicely by yourself. I wasn't needed."

She took his hand and brought it to her lips. "Oh, you were needed, all right. Very much needed."

In the aftermath of her struggle, Ellie began to drowse and then sleep, her head on his shoulder. But she never released his hand.

June sunlight spilled into the cabin as Ellie settled into sewing the new cotton sundress for Tanya. The old machine hummed smoothly, the material gliding beneath the needle.

This was Ellie's special place—intimate, small and filled with love. A place to think and resolve, to put the past behind her.

Adjusting to her new life took thought. Paul and Hillary would have to resolve their own lives and mistakes.

Paul had been silent, and with quiet pain, Ellie placed the little sister she had loved inside her heart—apart from the bitter, hurting selfish woman Hillary had become. Ellie had set firm rules with Hillary, keeping her at a distance. The separation of an older protective sister from a younger one wasn't easy; it hurt. But Hillary's decisions were her own, and when it was time, Ellie would tell Tanya of her biological mother and the choices the sisters had both made.

Mikhail's family had surrounded Ellie and Tanya with selfless love and understanding. Mary Jo held Ellie as she cried, understanding as only a woman could do as another moved through the passages of life and decision. Tanya moved easily between Mary Jo and Leigh and Bliss, thoroughly happy and carefree with the feminine blend, and obviously spoiled by the males—Fadey's "little princess." The Stepanovs' plain, honest talk, passions and hugs, the friendly taunts between brothers, the impromptu macho contests and Mary Jo's house rules for not breaking the furniture wrapped Ellie in a warm, beautiful life.

Fadey obviously delighted in Tanya and Katerina, showing them equal love. More than once, Mary Jo had hushed Fadey's wedding plans for Mikhail and Ellie. But Fadey's big bear hugs and grins said he couldn't wait long.

Mikhail waited, too. He'd never again mentioned marriage, but the question was in his sea-green eyes and in his silence at times.

Ellie felt tears burn her eyes and left her sewing to stand, looking at the letters from Nora—ones she had returned as mother and daughter gently grew to know each other.

The cabin was quiet, shadowed by Mikhail's love, and the new life before them. Understanding Ellie's need for privacy as she bridged her past and her future, the Stepanovs often kept Tanya—delighting in her—while Ellie came to the cabin with its spoon wind chimes and the sound of the endless waves.

The door between their suites was no longer closed. The rooms were a small home littered with Tanya's dolls and toys, a place for Ellie's sewing where Mikhail would sit nearby.

But in this cabin, Mikhail and Ellie made love in the soft nights, and she'd changed as a woman, with a woman's needs to make a home and to carry Mikhail's child.

Ellie's fingertip smoothed Nora's round script. Mother to daughter. Daughter to mother, ties as endless as the waves sliding onto the shore.

But there were other shadows in the past that Ellie wanted to remove.

If Kamakani's legendary curse was true, she'd dance before his grave, because she knew her heart, and her love for Mikhail. If there was a chance she could protect him from the painful past, she would....

He'd built the Amoteh, and if Paul forced him to, Mikhail would destroy it and build another competing resort. But that wasn't likely. Paul had called several times in the past month, carefully wedging questions about Ellie and Tanya's well-being into business. Those questions left no doubt in Mikhail that Paul was considering changing, to try to build some ties between his daughters and granddaughter—if he could. That was up to him.

In his office, Mikhail looked out the window and thought

of Ellie, slowly sorting her past and coming to know Nora. It was a hard journey, the edges troubling; but Ellie was strong—strong enough to distance herself from Hillary and Paul. Mikhail could only try to understand, and to wait—not an easy task for a man in love.

Mikhail frowned as he noted Ellie's mini-station wagon winding up the highway.

She never drove away from Amoteh—unless…

A half hour later, he found her car parked near the trail leading up to Kamakani's grave. He made his way slowly up the path, realizing that women made their own passages and a man shouldn't interfere. He could only wait and love.…

Mikhail paused on the edge of the forest, watching Ellie as she slowly undressed, dropping her clothing to a blanket.

There in front of Kamakani's grave, she stood tall, her arms raised to the sun, her body swaying, her feet moving gently over the lush grass.

It was an ancient dance, Mikhail knew, one that came from a woman's heart. Amid the silky swirl of her hair, the earrings he had given her caught the sun, sending out shards of gold.

And then Ellie turned to him, her body pale against the green trees. Her eyes were huge and solemn, holding a woman's wisdom and mystery. Her breasts were full and ripe and he'd known the pleasure of their soft weight, the taste. He'd known the curve of her waist, the jut of her bones, gentle flaring of her hips, the intimacy between her thighs, and the strength of her legs and arms.

He walked slowly toward her, jarred by the sensuality in the clear bright air, the primitive desire to take her instantly. His body throbbed almost painfully, needing hers, and then he caught her scent on the pine and salted breeze, arousing him even more.

Ellie's eyes were dark with passion, color riding her cheeks and yet she stood still and silent.

In his mind, he knew it was a woman's ritual he couldn't understand; he could only follow.

In his heart, he knew it was right—here and now and forever.

He undressed, his eyes never leaving hers. His hands trembled as they framed her face.

She tasted of woman and strength and love, moving against him, finding him with her thighs, lodging him there as they stood.

He tried to think, wanted to give Ellie the right words, and yet—yet he knew it was not the time. It was the time to become one, burning away everything else....

Ellie looked up at Mikhail as she lay on the blanket, welcoming him to her body. Mikhail was fierce and strong and gentle, always so gentle, even in his passions. Sunlight burnished his broad shoulders, his skin smooth over strong muscles and cords as he braced his full weight from her. His chest eased against her breasts, those searing green eyes traveling down to watch as her hips rose and they became one.

When he had undressed, his eyes never leaving hers, she'd known that their paths had always led here. She'd recognized the movements of his powerful body, the almost feline grace of a hunter, the slow, deliberate stride, his eyes as dark as the sea, his jaw locked as if nothing could keep him from her.

She needed this cleansing, here in the fresh scents of earth and pine and ocean, where the breeze would sweep away the clutter of life and leave the reality of their love.

Was she primitive? Demanding? Yes. Because he was hers. If there was a curse, she'd known her own heart, and she'd take Mikhail as her own.

There would be tender times—there had already been— between them, the quiet aftermath of love. Yet now, she wanted the cleansing fever, the burning away of the woman who had hurt him, and who would never touch their lives again. Ritualistic? Yes, but she needed this closure, to put the past away in lieu of a new life—together.

Whatever the other woman had taken from Mikhail, Ellie would fight fiercely to replace—because she loved him.

This time was different, Mikhail thought briefly, his body and heart already flowing with Ellie's, her dove-gray eyes locked with his as though she were fighting with all her strength, determined to win whatever war she waged.

Then he couldn't think anymore, his blood beating almost to primitive drums, the fiery storm begun as Ellie's fingers dug into his back, her body flowing, moist and hot against his. A song ran between them, their hearts pounding as they gave and took and feasted on each other, man and woman without shadows or the past....

The tempo had slowed, but Ellie's fierce needs drove her on. She reached to fist Mikhail's hair, tethering him. "Will you marry me?"

Mikhail's fierce sensual emotions slid into tenderness. He had once told her that she would have to ask him. "Of course."

"Will you give me a child?"

For just a moment, Mikhail's expression was wistful, but his soft uneven answer was typical Stepanov arrogance. "Of course."

And because she was Ellie, she pressed. "More than one?"

He could barely speak, fighting humble tears he did not want her to see. "A man can only try."

"Try again," she whispered and lifted to kiss him slowly, effectively. "I love you, you know."

Later, he would be able to speak, but for now, he would only tell her of his love in the simplest, truest of ways— by making love with her.

Epilogue

Mikhail poured pancake batter onto the hot griddle. The perfect mid-June morning outside the newly married Stepanovs' rented home was bright and clear and inside, he was at peace.

Strange, how a man could feel so good, so wonderful, cooking for his wife and Tanya while they snuggled in bed and talked. Women made a man's life good and rich and happy. He shrugged mentally, standing near the stove in his pajama bottoms that Ellie had sewn for him. He'd never asked what drove her to Kamakani's grave, but he knew—she fought to remove Kamakani's curse, to protect Mikhail and their love, just as other women had done before her.

While women had their secrets, Mikhail did not. The marriage he wanted as soon as possible was a flurry of preparation, with Ellie fussing over the dress she wanted, a traditional lacy Russian style, and Leigh, Bliss and Mary Jo in as much of a feminine flurry.

Their preparations gave the Stepanov men and Ed plenty

of time to consider house plans with a small pasture for
Tanya's new pony.

"It's a house. Just build it and soon. Oh, wait. Plan now,
we'll rent somewhere, and then we'll build it when business
slows down," Ellie had said as she rushed by him on the
way to talk with the florists. "Or, we can have a fall wedding and—"

"No," Mikhail had said firmly. "One week maximum."

"I want this wedding to be done right. You're pushing.
It takes time, you know. Four weeks."

"Two weeks, no more." Mikhail had eased her into a
storage closet and did his best to convince her why he
wanted her in his bed every night, not just when they could
find the time. "You're not always going to get away with
that, Mr. Stepanov," she'd whispered huskily. "You're
sexy and you know it."

"I want you in my bed every night, married as my wife.
Is that so much to ask?"

She'd quivered and held him tight. "No, it isn't. I want
you, too."

Strange, Mikhail thought as he turned the pancakes, how
a woman gentled a man's storms. How she could walk to
him in the church, her hand in her mother's, dressed in lace
and love, and take away his breath.

He'd remember her like that always, even when they
aged—walking toward him in the flower-decked church
aisle, her eyes so soft and filled with tears. Or were those
his tears?

Mikhail smiled briefly as he sat the table. Or maybe they
were Fadey's and Jarek's tears, because he was not alone
in his tender emotions.

He placed his hands on his hips and critically studied the
breakfast he had prepared—butter, syrup, jam, coffee and
juice.

In a few months, he would carry Ellie into their new
home, filled with good Stepanov furniture, made to last.
And the showroom bed where they spent their first night

together was already theirs, holding a special sentiment for Mikhail. "Life is good," he said quietly. "I am a man who has everything—"

A tiny feminine flurry of tousled hair, a cotton nightie, arms and legs, Tanya ran into the kitchen and threw herself at him.

Mikhail laughed and picked her up, lifting her high the way she liked and then placing her on his hip. Tanya's small hand patted his cheek. "Hey, Dad?"

"Mmm?" Mikhail answered, but his mind was spinning. "Dad" was a wonderful word, a glorious name.

"Dad, Mom has a surprise for you. She's worried you might get morning sickness if she told you—you wouldn't, would you? She said it's a very nice secret that only she knows and very, very new. Something that got made on your wedding night. She's going to tell me in about two or three months."

"A Stepanov is never sick— Ah…" Mikhail slowly realized the impact of Tanya's news. "I…uh…think I have to sit down."

With Tanya on his lap, Mikhail felt woozy and delighted and— He looked up to see Ellie leaning against the door frame, smirking beautifully at him.

"I am delighted, of course," he said very formally when he could speak.

"I love you, big guy," Ellie said quietly and Mikhail couldn't stop looking at her, his love, his wife.

"I'm hungry," Tanya said, leaping out of arms and scooting into her place at the table.

"Life goes on, Stepanov. Food, babies, family, kids, and the pony has to be fed. We'll conference later, okay?" Ellie came to pat him on the head, then bent to kiss him. "Feeling better?"

"Much better," Mikhail said with a widening grin as he felt as if he could float, wallow in whatever life brought him with Ellie. "How could I not?"

*   *   *   *   *

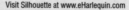

If you enjoyed what you just read,
then we've got an offer you can't resist!

Take 2 bestselling love stories FREE!
Plus get a FREE surprise gift!

Clip this page and mail it to Silhouette Reader Service™

IN U.S.A.	IN CANADA
3010 Walden Ave.	P.O. Box 609
P.O. Box 1867	Fort Erie, Ontario
Buffalo, N.Y. 14240-1867	L2A 5X3

YES! Please send me 2 free Silhouette Desire® novels and my free surprise gift. After receiving them, if I don't wish to receive anymore, I can return the shipping statement marked cancel. If I don't cancel, I will receive 6 brand-new novels every month, before they're available in stores! In the U.S.A., bill me at the bargain price of $3.57 plus 25¢ shipping and handling per book and applicable sales tax, if any*. In Canada, bill me at the bargain price of $4.24 plus 25¢ shipping and handling per book and applicable taxes**. That's the complete price and a savings of at least 10% off the cover prices—what a great deal! I understand that accepting the 2 free books and gift places me under no obligation ever to buy any books. I can always return a shipment and cancel at any time. Even if I never buy another book from Silhouette, the 2 free books and gift are mine to keep forever.

225 SDN DNUP
326 SDN DNUQ

Name	(PLEASE PRINT)	
Address	Apt.#	
City	State/Prov.	Zip/Postal Code

* Terms and prices subject to change without notice. Sales tax applicable in N.Y.
** Canadian residents will be charged applicable provincial taxes and GST.
All orders subject to approval. Offer limited to one per household and not valid to current Silhouette Desire® subscribers.
® are registered trademarks of Harlequin Books S.A., used under license.

DES02   ©1998 Harlequin Enterprises Limited

Don't miss the latest miniseries from award-winning author Marie Ferrarella:

The MOM SQUAD

Meet...

Sherry Campbell—ambitious newswoman who makes headlines when a handsome billionaire arrives to sweep her off her feet...and shepherd her new son into the world!
A BILLIONAIRE AND A BABY, SE#1528, available March 2003

Joanna Prescott—Nine months after her visit to the sperm bank, her old love rescues her from a burning house—then delivers her baby....
A BACHELOR AND A BABY, SD#1503, available April 2003

Chris "C.J." Jones—FBI agent, expectant mother and always on the case. When the baby comes, will her irresistible partner be by her side?
THE BABY MISSION, IM#1220, available May 2003

Lori O'Neill—A forbidden attraction blows down this pregnant Lamaze teacher's tough-woman facade and makes her consider the love of a lifetime!
BEAUTY AND THE BABY, SR#1668, available June 2003

The Mom Squad—these single mothers-to-be are ready for labor...and true love!

Silhouette®
Where love comes alive™

The secret is out!

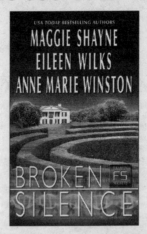

Coming in May 2003 to SILHOUETTE BOOKS

Evidence has finally surfaced that a covert team
of scientists successfully completed experiments
in genetic manipulation.

The extraordinary individuals created by these
experiments could be anyone, living anywhere,
even right next door....

Enjoy these three brand-new FAMILY SECRETS
stories and watch as dark pasts are exposed
and passion burns through the night!

The Invisible Virgin by Maggie Shayne
A Matter of Duty by Eileen Wilks
Inviting Trouble by Anne Marie Winston

Five extraordinary siblings. One dangerous past.

Visit Silhouette at www.eHarlequin.com   PSBS

COMING NEXT MONTH

#1507 WHERE THERE'S SMOKE...—Barbara McCauley
Dynasties: The Barones
Emily Barone couldn't remember anything—except for the fireman
who'd saved her life. Soft-spoken and innocent, she had no defenses against
Shane Cummings's bone-melting charm. Before she knew it, she'd given him
her body and her heart. But would she trade her Barone riches to find happily-
ever-after with her real-life hero?

#1508 THE GENTRYS: CINCO—Linda Conrad
The Gentrys
The last thing rancher Cinco Gentry needed was a beautiful, headstrong retired
air force captain disrupting his well-ordered life. But when a crazed killer
threatened Meredith Powell, Cinco agreed to let her stay with him. And though
Meredith's independent ways continually clashed with his protective streak,
Cinco realized he, too, was in danger—of falling for his feisty houseguest!

#1509 CHEROKEE BABY—Sheri WhiteFeather
A whirlwind affair had left Julianne McKenzie with one giant surprise.... She
was pregnant with ranch owner Bobby Elk's baby. The sexy Cherokee was not
in the market for marriage but, once he learned Julianne carried his child, he
quickly offered her a permanent place in his life. Yet Julianne would only
settle for *all* of her Cherokee lover's heart.

#1510 SLEEPING WITH BEAUTY—Laura Wright
Living alone in the Colorado Rockies, U.S. Marshal Dan Mason didn't want
company, especially of the drop-dead-gorgeous variety. But when a hiking
accident left violet-eyed "Angel" on his doorstep with no memory and no
identity, he took her in. Dan had closed off his heart years ago—could this
mysterious beauty bring him back to life?

#1511 THE COWBOY'S BABY BARGAIN—Emilie Rose
The Baby Bank
Brooke Blake's biological clock was ticking, so she struck an irresistible
bargain with tantalizing cowboy Caleb Lander. The deal? She'd give him back
his family's land if he fathered her baby! But Brooke had no inkling that their
arrangement would be quite so pleasurable, and she ached to keep this
heartstoppingly handsome rancher in her bed and in her life.

#1512 HER CONVENIENT MILLIONAIRE—Gail Dayton
Desperate to escape an arranged marriage, Sherry Nyland needed a temporary
husband—fast! Millionaire Micah Scott could never resist a damsel in distress,
so when Sherry proposed a paper marriage, he agreed to help her. But it wasn't
long before Micah was falling for his lovely young bride. Now he just had to
convince Sherry that he intended to love, honor and cherish her...forever!

SDCNM0403